"We're friends. I value that more than I do a passing romance,"

Jake told Joanna.

"And passing is all it would be?"

Jake looked directly into her luminous eyes. "That's all either of us has ever known."

"But our friendship—"

"Is something I don't want to lose, Jo. And we will," he said, reaching out and caressing her cheek, "if we let this happen."

His eyes, dark with anguish, mesmerized her. She raised a hand, her fingers covering his where they touched her face.

"I'm sorry, Jo."

She took a deep breath of reality. This was the end of whatever she'd hoped for. It felt final. Painful, but final, and maybe that was good. Jake couldn't make his heart feel something it just wouldn't feel.

Books by Kathryn Alexander

Love Inspired

The Reluctant Bride #18
A Wedding in the Family #42
The Forever Husband #78
Twin Wishes #96
Heart of a Husband #116

KATHRYN ALEXANDER

writes inspirational romance because, having been a Christian for many years, incorporating the element of faith in the Lord into a romantic story line seemed like a lovely and appropriate idea. After all, in a society where love for a lifetime is difficult to find, imagine discovering it, unexpectedly, as a gift sent from God.

Kathryn is married to Kelly, her own personal love of a lifetime. They have one son, John, who is the proud owner of the family's two house pests, Herbie the cat and Copper the dog.

Kathryn and her family have been members of their church for nearly five years, where she co-teaches a Sunday school class of active two-year-olds. She is now a stay-at-home mom who writes between car pooling, baby-sitting and applying bandages, when necessary.

Heart of a Husband
Kathryn Alexander

Love Inspired

Published by Steeple Hill Books™

STEEPLE HILL BOOKS

Steeple Hill™

ISBN 0-373-87122-8

HEART OF A HUSBAND

Copyright © 2000 by Kathryn Leatherwood

The boundary lines have fallen for me
in pleasant places.

—*Psalms* 16:6a

Chapter One

"Joanna."

She heard her name spoken quietly from some-where behind her as she stood speaking with a nurse in the pale blues and greens of the hospital waiting room. Her breath caught in her throat momentarily. There was no need to turn around to see who had spoken; she remembered his voice clearly. It sounded exactly as it had two years ago, when he'd said good-bye. Closing her eyes for a brief moment, she wondered what she would say. Then she turned.

A well-cut suit, the color of charcoal, accentuated his tall, lean frame, and the faded remnant of a tan stood out in contrast to the crisp whiteness of his shirt. Looking up, Joanna's velvet-brown eyes met cautious gray.

"Hello, Jake," she managed to say. "It's nice of you to come." She extended a slender hand to him.

"It's good to see you," he answered in a voice low

and achingly familiar. He clasped her hand in a necessary handshake. "How is Mae?"

"Not good," Joanna responded. "Dr. Eden is with her now, but you can see her in a few minutes."

"And you?"

"Fine. I'm fine," she responded, a little too quickly, she realized.

"Are you?" came his immediate reply. The slate-gray depths of his eyes, genuinely sad, held her gaze easily. "You look tired."

"I'm all right," she replied. "Tired, but okay."

"It's been a long time," Jake remarked.

"Yes," she agreed. But had it been too long? Or not long enough? The ache in her heart made it difficult to think, difficult to do anything other than feel.

"I want to help, Jo. That's why I'm here."

Joanna nodded her head without speaking. Dr. Jake Barnes's help was exactly what she didn't want. For him to show up now—kind and caring—was what she had feared. Comfort from Jake now would be more than she could endure. The memories she had spent long months pushing to the back of her mind stirred again in her thoughts. All of the forgetting could too easily be undone.

Joanna glanced toward the nearby hospital room to see Dr. Natalie Eden, Mae's family physician, walking toward them where they stood in the lobby.

"Natalie, how are you?" Jake spoke directly to the attractive physician who smiled broadly when she saw him.

"Jake! I wasn't sure you'd come. It's wonderful to see you," Dr. Eden said just as Joanna stepped away, excusing herself from the scene to return to her aunt's bedside. A warm, welcoming embrace between these two people was more than she could handle at the moment. Dr. Jake Barnes and Dr. Natalie Eden. There had been a brief time, years ago, when they'd seemed the perfect couple in everyone's eyes. Including Joanna's. Until her own heart had found reason to think otherwise.

"'To be absent from the body is to be present with the Lord,'" was the scripture her aunt whispered in a weak voice as Joanna entered the room. Those were the first words Mae had spoken all day.

"Yes," Joanna agreed. "I know that's always been one of your favorite verses." She sank into a chair close to the bed and reached for the elderly woman's hand. "But I'd rather keep you here with me. I'm not ready to let you go," she added as she saw her aunt's eyes fluttering shut again.

"Jake is here?" Mae asked in wispy words.

"Yes, he's here," Joanna answered.

Mae gave a small smile. "He said he'd come. He'll take care of everything. He'll take care of you, Joanna."

"I don't need taking care of," Joanna said with a soft moan of protest. She tucked some of her ash-blond hair behind an ear. "I'm all grown-up, Aunt Mae. I can take care of myself."

But her aunt had already drifted back to sleep, just as she had done off and on for the past few days. Joanna studied the dull gold wedding band on her aunt's finger. What would it be like, she wondered, to love a man the way Mae had loved her husband?

To remain true to him, committed to him even many years after his death? A love of that depth was rare, Joanna knew, but she believed it was as possible as it was rare.

Giving a soft sigh, she placed Mae's cool, frail hand against her own cheek. So, Jake had decided to come back to say goodbye to Mae. That shouldn't have surprised her, she knew. Aunt Mae had been like a mother to them both, each in different ways. Jake would want to be here. As a doctor, a friend, the son Mae wanted but never had. Jake would be what Mae needed. He was good at that. And Joanna would have to pretend she didn't need him, too.

"Lord, don't take her away from me yet. I'm not ready for that," she breathed the heartfelt prayer.

It seemed a long time ago, but it had been only four years earlier—just as Joanna was starting college—that she had accepted Mae's invitation to live with her in South Carolina. She had arrived at her aunt's house with suitcases in hand and much hope in her heart. Joanna had been grateful for Mae's offer after years of growing up in an adoptive home where she felt very much an outsider. Mae was the only biological link Joanna Meccord had to the past after losing her parents in a plane crash as a child. Early one spring afternoon, a cabdriver had left Joanna at the specified address, Mae's house. And Jake was there, even that first day. Living in Charleston then, he worked at a clinic not far from Mae's home, and had just finished having lunch with Mae when Joanna rang the doorbell. Joanna smiled as she recalled the latch on one of the suitcases Jake carried in for her breaking as he placed it next to the hallway closet. They had knelt together on the carpeting, gathering up books and belongings that had tumbled from the luggage while Joanna silently thanked the Lord that it had been this bag that had broken. Not the one holding more personal items. The breaking of the old, battered bag was inevitable, Joanna had explained quickly, and it was not worth repairing as Jake offered to have done. She remembered his smile. A half smile, not particularly disarming enough to set her heart to hammering, but it had been nice. The smile of a friend.

Those opening, awkward moments were the beginning of her life with Aunt Mae and a relationship with Dr. Jake Barnes. And their casual friendship was reinforced when days later, a present for Joanna was delivered to Mae's front door: two new pieces of floral tapestry luggage with a card attached. It read, "Joanna, For your next move, which I hope is many years from now. Jake."

Joanna's friendship with him deepened throughout her college years. Jake's curiosity about her Christian faith and their common concern for Mae's failing health helped weave an unspoken bond between them. Not even Mae's hints that she thought the new clinic physician, Natalie Eden, was a perfect match for Jake had bothered Joanna then. Through all this and more, Joanna and Jake remained simply friends, sharing bits and pieces of knowing each other without really knowing each other at all. Until one gentle evening when their friendship was lost in an unguarded moment. And everything changed.

Soon Jake was gone. Suddenly and unexpectedly, he moved away, and Dr. Natalie Eden was quick to do the explaining. It seemed Jake had wanted Natalie to move back to Indiana with him so he could take over his father's private practice. He wanted to return to the home of his childhood, and when Natalie had turned him down, he left without her.

So Jake was gone, and Joanna had tried to forget— the hello, the goodbye. And everything in between.

"Jo?"

She looked up immediately at the sound of Jake's voice coming from the doorway of Mae's hospital room.

"May I come in?" Jake asked and watched Joanna nod her head. Her loose hair swayed gently with the easy movement. If only he couldn't remember how soft those blond curls felt in his hands, against his face. He cleared his throat quietly and walked over to Mae's bedside. Leaning down, he brushed a kiss against the elderly woman's forehead as she slept. "She doesn't want to die, Jo. She's very worried about leaving you alone."

"How would you know that?" she asked softly.

Jake sat down next to Mae, wishing he were any-where but here, now, having this discussion. Joanna looked so unhappy. So distant, worried. He hated knowing that his words would only make her sadder. "Mae told me when I saw her last week."

"You were in town last week?" Joanna repeated, her dark-brown eyes wide with question.

"I was here for a few hours," he explained what he'd not wanted to tell Joanna. That he'd come this far, flown from Indianapolis to Charleston, but not to see her. "I visited Mae, met with her cardiologist and Dr. Eden and caught a late-afternoon flight home. I had to be back for a meeting that night."

"But she didn't tell me, she never mentioned it," Joanna practically whispered in disbelief.

"I want to take her home with me, Joanna. To live."

"To die, you mean," she replied.

"I hope not," he remarked.

Joanna breathed a frustrated sigh. "Dr. Eden said Aunt Mae is going to die. Soon. Why would you want to put her through the stress of traveling nearly seven hundred miles now, when it's too late?"

"I've spoken with Mae's doctors, Joanna, and I don't think she's getting the kind of care she needs. My partner at the office, Dr. Vernon, has a brother who is the leading cardiologist in this half of the country. If anyone can make a difference in Mae's life, it will be him. I want her to see him, to come and stay with me for as long as it takes."

"But Dr. Eden told me she has so little time left—"

"That's all she'll have if you keep her here. If she goes with me, I think she could have more. Weeks, maybe months. Or longer."

"But, Jake, the move alone could kill her."

"I don't believe it will, but she's going to die here, in this hospital, if we do nothing. I want her to come with me. Tonight," he responded. "I've made arrangements for the flight."

"You can't take her away from me, Jake. Not now.

She's all I have left in this world. I can't believe this would be the Lord's will for her life...her death...."

The anguish in her voice pierced Jake's conscience. He knew how much this hurt her. That's why he hated the promise he'd made. "You can't let her die here, like this...always wondering if you did all you could for her. No one wants to live with those doubts." He paused. "I don't want you living with those doubts, Joanna."

"But she's comfortable here, she's not in any pain—"

"Give her this chance, Jo. Let her see this new cardiologist."

"But I don't know if she'd want to make this move, Jake. I mean, I know she was born and raised in Indiana, just like you were, but that doesn't mean she wants to go there to die. Does it?"

Jake exhaled slowly. There was no avoiding this now. "It's what she wants, Joanna. It's what she asked me to promise I would do...and she's appointed me her power of attorney," he said quietly, reluctantly. He'd hoped Mae had taken care of explaining the matter to Joanna. Telling her himself reopened wounds he'd never intended to inflict. This would cut through Joanna like a betrayal.

"So, basically, you can do whatever you want, regardless of how I feel about it?" she asked, clearly surprised by this unexpected piece of news.

"I don't want to go against your wishes, Jo. You have to know that. But—" He stopped.

"But you will?" she asked, her eyes glimmering with fresh tears. "Jake? You'd take her away from

me? Like this?'' Joanna's hand flew to her mouth.
"How could you? Don't you care—"

"Of course, I care," Jake answered with a heaviness settling in his chest. Why had he promised to do
this? Then he reminded himself of his reasoning.
There'd been logic in it, even in the midst of the
heartbreak. "Your Aunt Mae is the closest I've ever
come to having a mother in my life. I can provide a
better ending for her than this."

Joanna rose from her chair, hugging her arms close
as a chill swept over her. "Money, Jake?" she asked
sadly. "Is that what this comes down to? You're
wealthy so you can come in here and take her away?"
Her words were filled with pain. It glistened in the
murky depths of her eyes.

"It's more than that." Jake's dark brows drew into
a troubled frown. "It's true I can provide better care,
but I'm only trying to do what I promised I would
do. Help me with this, Jo, while there's still time.
Don't hate me for doing what needs to be done."

"Hate you?" She almost wished she could. Then
life would be simple again. Black and white. No more
gray areas to wander around in. Alone.

"And I wouldn't be taking her away from you,"
Jake added before delivering what he knew would be
the final blow to her shaken emotions. "She wants
you to come, too."

"What?" she asked, too stunned to say more.

Jake squeezed Mae's hand gently before moving
from her bedside. "She loves you...she needs you.
She wants you with her." He glanced back into
Joanna's bewildered gaze. "You'll need to think it

over, I know, but we don't have much time," he said.
"I'll leave you alone for a while." Then he walked
away, disappearing through the door, leaving Joanna
standing there, her mouth open in surprise.

For a moment, she couldn't move, couldn't even
think clearly. Had Jake really said that she should go
with him? To Indiana? Had he lost his mind? Or just
his memory of why that would never work? She
turned on her heels to follow him out into the hallway
where she found him speaking with Dr. Eden.

"Jake," she interrupted. "I can't go away like that.
Just pack up and leave? Are you serious?"

"Very," Jake answered, directing his attention toward Joanna. He excused them from the other physician's presence and cupped Joanna's elbow with a
hand, steering her toward the privacy of an empty
lobby. "I know you weren't expecting any of this,
but Mae asked me to promise that you'd go, too. And
I did." He glanced down at the discharge papers Dr.
Eden had handed him and then back into Joanna's
panic-filled eyes. "It's what she wants, Jo." He
paused, never so uncertain of anything in his life as
he was of this. He wanted Joanna to go with him more
than he dared to admit but, at the same time, he
couldn't calculate the magnitude of mistake they
would be making. Still, he'd made the promise.
"There's a flight at seven—"

"Seven o'clock? Tonight?" Joanna asked.

"Yes," Jake replied. "You won't need to pack
much. We're having a rough winter back home. You
can buy warmer clothes when you get there."

With what? she wondered. Joanna didn't have extra

money for winter clothing. She hadn't even had enough in her checking account to pay her school bill last semester.

Money. Joanna nearly cringed at the thought. The power of it, the need of it, the control it wielded. And all it had cost her. It was the private plane of a rich corporate executive that had crashed and taken the lives of her parents long ago. They'd been flying in inclement weather to meet the demanding schedule of a client they deemed important enough to take necessary risks for. The "necessary risk" that day took their lives when the plane went nose down into a lake.

Now, Jake and his money would be able to take Aunt Mae away to die in some strange house, in a state the woman hadn't visited since childhood. It wasn't fair.

"Joanna, is seven o'clock okay? I could send a cab for you—"

"No, it's not okay," she replied. "I need to get out of here. I want some fresh air," she said suddenly and bolted for the nearby exit. The cool, damp weather felt good on her warm cheeks. She took a deep breath just as the doors opened behind her.

"Joanna, I know this isn't easy for you."

"No, it's not." She turned to face him, her fists clenched at her sides. "I can't go to Indiana with you, Jake. I can't stay with you and you know it, so why ask? Just to embarrass me?"

An honest look of surprise flashed in his eyes. "I would never try to embarrass you. What are you talking about?"

She flung her hands out in despair. "We're not a

good match. Not in any way. You've made that clear enough. You feel it, I feel it. I think even God feels that way about us. Putting us in the same house together for any amount of time will only lead to…to…arguments. Or worse." A sinking feeling weighted the pit of her stomach.

Raking a hand through his dark hair, Jake turned away from her. She was right. He couldn't dispute the truth. But, somehow, they had to get beyond it temporarily to help Mae. To keep a promise. He placed both hands on the metal railing that surrounded the veranda. "Joanna, I'm sorry. Sorry we went out alone together on your birthday, sorry about everything that happened." He hesitated. "I shouldn't have touched you."

"I don't want your apology," she said quickly. What she wanted now, and a hundred times since that night, was to be in his arms again. And she was angry at herself for wanting this man who didn't want her, not even when she'd foolishly been there for the taking. She watched Jake turn his head to glance at her. His wistful look tugged at the sweet ache in her heart.

"I can't force you to come home with me, Jo. You're twenty-two years old, old enough to make your own decisions." He paused for a moment. "But it's what Mae wants. It's what she needs."

"She shouldn't expect such a thing of me. She doesn't have any idea how awkward it would be."

"You didn't tell her that things…had changed between us?" Jake studied her restless movements as she inched a little farther from him.

"No, I didn't," she acknowledged. Joanna folded

her arms together. "It didn't seem right. She would have blamed you."

"She should have blamed me," he responded, his voice filled with regret. "I was thirty-two years old. You were barely twenty."

Joanna shivered at the thought of that night's misery. "When you left me at my door in tears, I felt like I was about eight."

"I wish you had been," he said with a sad smile, then averted his gaze to the darkening skies. "Then I could have been trusted to take you to dinner and return you home safely, with your heart in one piece."

"I was safe with you, Jake," she responded. Incredibly, agonizingly safe, Joanna remembered. "Only my pride was hurt." She rubbed the chill away from her arms when their eyes met again. The tenderness in his gaze only deepened her sense of loneliness.

"I'm sorry, Jo," he offered gently. Sorry most of all that he had unwittingly let this lovely young woman find a way into the heart he'd kept cold and silent all those years. His father's sorrows had taught him well. How not to trust. Not to love. But with Joanna... Nothing made sense anymore.

Biting her lip, Joanna looked away. "It wasn't something I couldn't get over," she lied as her pulse pounded with guilt. She wasn't going to let him know how badly it had hurt, how badly it still hurt—even now. Maybe God would forgive her this little lie, this one indiscretion.

"There's no need to be afraid that—"

"I'm not afraid," Joanna stated. Indiscretion number two. She was afraid. Of them. Of all they would never be together.

Jake studied her thoughtfully before transferring his gaze to the setting sun in the distance. If she didn't agree to go, then this would be the end of it. He couldn't go through this again. Seeing her sad. Lovely. And so alone.

A silence fell between them momentarily that hung heavy like a cloud. When Jake spoke again, his words were gentle. "Come home with me, Jo."

Joanna swallowed hard, feeling as if her heart had jumped into her throat. What should she do? What was the right choice? What would the Lord expect of her? Only one thing was certain. If she didn't go with him, she might never see Aunt Mae again. Never.

"Are you sure about this, Jake? Absolutely sure it's…the right thing…to do?" She was stalling, she knew. Waiting, wanting something more from him than she'd seen.

"Yes," he responded with a confidence he didn't feel. "It's what Mae wants, and it's what I want." But the thin, straight line of his mouth offered no hint of the emotions storming inside him.

Joanna shivered, although the damp air was not cool enough to justify it. If she was going to make this journey, she'd need God's guidance every step of the way. Otherwise, it would be a huge mistake. A journey she'd get lost in. One she'd regret. There'd be no relying on herself this time. She took a quiet breath as her mind raced with a crazy blend of hope and fear.

"All right," she told him. She'd go. A risk taker wasn't something Joanna had considered herself to be, but people could change. Especially in the face of great loss. Couldn't they?

Jake nodded. A mixture of feelings surged through him, none of which he could voice. Everything from the satisfaction of winning an argument to the uneasiness of facing the truth of what he'd just lost. A chance to walk away from this woman who haunted his dreams. Was that what he'd wanted?

"Let's go inside," Jake said. They stepped off the veranda and walked back through the double doors of the hospital. "I'll be leaving with Mae at seven."

"But, Jake, I can't be ready by then. There are things I need to do, people I need to call. I'll have to notify the day care center where I work." Excuses poured from Joanna.

"I understand," Jake conceded. "I guess that would be a lot to ask. I'll see about getting you a flight on another day."

"All right," she agreed. "I'll get everything taken care of as quickly as I can."

"I'll ask my housekeeper to call you later with your flight information. That is, unless you don't want to fly," Jake began and then hesitated, searching Joanna's face for the truth he expected. "I know that your parents died in a plane crash. If you'd rather not fly, I'll make other arrangements."

"No," Joanna replied. "I don't mind. I flew several times with my adoptive parents when I was a child."

"You're sure?" he asked.

She nodded her head.

"Okay, then, I'll make the necessary arrangements to move Mae tonight."

"And you'll go with her? I mean, be right there, with her? The whole time?"

"Yes. She'll be comfortable," Jake explained. "Don't worry, Jo. I'll be right beside her bed the entire trip. You'll see her again soon."

"You'll take good care of her?"

"I will," he promised as they continued walking down the corridor. "Trust me."

Joanna turned her head to glance into eyes she used to trust. Did she have reason to trust them no longer?

They were nearing Mae's hospital room when Dr. Eden appeared in the hallway again, needing Dr. Barnes's opinion on some matter. Something crucial, Joanna thought unkindly, like whether he would be staying to have dinner with her tonight, maybe? If Dr. Eden didn't want to marry Jake Barnes when she had the opportunity, why was she now so obviously delighted to see him? A change of heart, probably, just as Joanna had always expected. The only surprise was that it had been so long in coming.

Joanna slipped into the silent hospital room to say good-night to her aunt before heading home. There was so much to do in preparation for leaving, she barely knew where to begin. But she had to start somewhere, so upon her arrival at the small house she shared with Mae, Joanna hauled her suitcases out of a bedroom closet. What a place to start, she thought as she sat down on the edge of her bed.

"Lord, what am I doing?" She sat staring at the

suitcases Jake had given her when she'd been practically a stranger to him. Was she really going to fill
them with clothes and get on that plane? To meet Jake
in some strange city in a state she'd never seen? To
move into his house? Had she lost all rational thinking?

"Probably," she whispered. Reason seemed to
have disappeared somewhere behind the shadows of
her heart.

Chapter Two

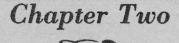

"Joanna? Joanna Meccord, is that you?"

Joanna turned from the baggage claim area toward the direction of the voice and found the question coming from a plump, silver-haired lady.

"I'm Joanna Meccord," she confirmed.

"I thought so. Dr. Barnes gave a very good description."

Joanna smiled. Jake describing her to someone. Now, there was something she'd have been interested in hearing. "So, you must be Jake's housekeeper?" she asked.

"Yes, I'm Ina Marsh. Second generation housekeeper as a matter of fact. I worked for Dr. Barnes, Sr., for several years until he passed away. And now I work for Jake. He'd planned to meet you here himself, but an emergency came up at the hospital and he couldn't get away. So I offered to pick you up," the woman with the friendly smile and kind hazel eyes explained. She reached to take one of Joanna's suitcases.

"No, you don't. I'll carry these, Ina, you just lead the way out of this airport."

"Right over there, dear," Ina said, and they started through the lobby. After a few long minutes, they found their way to a sea of cars in the parking lot. Ina stopped behind a small blue sedan.

"How is Aunt Mae?" Joanna asked. "Is someone with her?"

"Oh, my, yes. Someone is always with her. Dr. Barnes wouldn't allow it to be any other way. There's a nurse there right now. Occasionally, it's just me, but usually there's an RN or LPN on duty. Didn't you bring more than this, dear?" Ina asked as Joanna lifted the two suitcases into the trunk.

"No, this is it. Is Aunt Mae feeling any better?"

"Yes, I think she is. She was talking this morning. She said she's glad to be home. She was born and raised around here, she told me. Looking out her bedroom window and seeing acres of farmland does her good—even though there isn't any corn growing in late February! 'The boundary lines have fallen for me in pleasant places….' That's a verse she asked me to write down inside the cover of her Bible. I guess rural Indiana must be her idea of 'pleasant places.'"

Joanna got into the car just as Ina was sliding into the driver's seat. "I've always liked that verse."

"It seems to be one of her favorites," Ina commented. "Dr. Barnes told me you're a religious person, too. I assumed he meant you're a Christian."

"Yes," Joanna answered. "Although some days I

don't feel like much of one. Between Aunt Mae's illness and everything else I've been trying to keep up with, I haven't been to church regularly in weeks.''

"Well, don't be too hard on yourself. God understands what you're going through. And everyone makes mistakes.''

Was that what she was doing now? Making a huge mistake? Joanna's teeth sank gently into her lower lip. Living with Jake could be the biggest error she'd ever made. Yet, here she was with a conscience that had a guilty edge to it. She knew she wasn't doing this just for Mae. It was for herself, too. Her feelings for Jake needed to be resolved. Completely. Because, despite her prayers to the contrary, Jake did not seem to be the man the Lord had in mind for her. Now, if she could just convince her heart of that fact.

"I've been instructed that our first stop is the nearest shopping mall to buy a winter coat and whatever other clothes you need. Today is an exceptionally mild day for February, but let me warn you—it gets cold around here!'' Ina explained.

Joanna knew exactly how much money she had brought with her, and it wasn't enough to allow for the purchase of any new clothing. "Ina, I don't think that—''

"Now, listen, Dr. Barnes told me you wouldn't want to accept this, but my instructions were to talk you into it. So, please make it easy on me, okay, dear? He wants you to buy a coat, hat, boots, whatever else you need. He gave me these credit cards.''

Joanna immediately protested. "Ina, I can't accept—''

"My job is to give them to you. Now, if you don't want to keep them, you'll have to argue with the doctor about that."

And argue, she knew she would.

They were soon leaving the city behind, traveling down narrow country roads with their necessary purchases completed. Joanna spent the time wondering about things to come. Hopefully, Aunt Mae would recuperate enough to return to South Carolina soon. If not, then what? Joanna liked plans, lists—knowing what came next—and she certainly wasn't in that position now.

Before long they made one last turn and pulled into the winding, tree-lined driveway in full view of the farmhouse.

The large white house was nestled among several wooded acres of gently rolling farmland. A two-story barn, garage and a couple of other small buildings were set off to the rear and the west side of the home, and a white board fence neatly edged the property line.

"I had no idea it would be so lovely," Joanna said.

"It is, isn't it," Ina replied. She pulled the car up close to the garage, and both of them got out of the vehicle.

Joanna looked toward the woods, now stark and barren from the harshness of winter.

"Just wait until you see it in the summer, Joanna. The trees will be beautiful then."

"I can almost imagine it," she said, hugging her new coat to her in the hush of the late-winter afternoon. "But I won't be here this summer," she added before pulling her suitcases from the trunk of the car and walking with Ina toward the front porch.

"You never know what the good Lord might have in mind for you, my dear. We'll just have to wait and see, won't we?"

Joanna was ready to respond that, whatever the Lord had in mind for her, it certainly wouldn't include a future with a man who loved neither her nor God, when Ina began describing the house.

"Upstairs there are four bedrooms and four bathrooms."

"Four baths? Are you kidding?"

"Not at all," Ina assured her. "I heard Jake's mother entertained a lot years ago. She wanted each bedroom to have a private bath. And, this, as you can see, is the main entrance." They stepped inside the home. "The living room is to your right."

They walked into the large room with warm, inviting tones of gold, rust and shades of brown throughout.

Ina continued, "That door to the left at the foot of the staircase is Dr. Barnes's study. Lately, he's been spending too many of his evenings in there, if you ask me."

Joanna smiled. The fact that she hadn't asked Ina's opinion obviously didn't stop the woman from giving it. "Jake probably wants to be alone," Joanna replied. She wondered if he regretted this mission of mercy he'd set into motion to help Aunt Mae. It was costing him much more than money.

"Well, I'm hoping that your arrival will put an end

to his being alone so much. It's not good for him. I've only been staying here for a few days. Until then, he lived in this great big old house all by himself. Can you imagine that?''

Yes, Joanna could imagine that. But she smiled and shook her head. There wasn't much point in defending Jake. He enjoyed solitude, whether Ina understood that or not. "So, that's the dining room?''

"Yes," Ina responded, looking into the adjoining room. But Dr. Barnes prefers to eat in the kitchen usually. Let's go upstairs so I can show you your room.''

They climbed the staircase together. "That's yours there to the left," Ina explained when they reached the top. "Mine is right across the hallway. Aunt Mae is in that room down on the right, and the fourth is a guest room. Dr. Barnes has the master bedroom, which is downstairs next to the study.

"Let me put these suitcases in here, then I'll go see Aunt Mae." Joanna stepped inside the door to her room and stopped. *Exquisite* was the only word that came to mind. She looked from the delicate furniture fashioned from honey-colored oak to the soft, pale colors of the wallpaper with matching curtains and bedspread. Realistic oil paintings of Victorian gardens and English cottages hung over two dressers. In the far corner near a window, there was an overstuffed chair covered in tapestrylike fabric similar to the paintings.

"Well, do you like it?'' Ina asked.

"It's wonderful. Amazing," Joanna replied, stunned to find such lavish surroundings. Several times during her unsettled childhood, she had walked into a new home, a new bedroom—but nothing as lovely as this had ever awaited her.

"I told Dr. Barnes you would. I helped with the decorating," Ina answered with a grin. "Now, let's get you down the hallway to see your aunt."

And down the hallway they went. Joanna found her aunt awake, with a little more color in her face than the last time she'd seen her and very happy to see her niece again.

It was much later that afternoon before Joanna unpacked her clothes and then eased into the ivory porcelain tub for a bath. She leaned her head back, soaking her hair as she sank into the vanilla-scented bubbles. For the first time in weeks, she didn't rush through her bath to hurry over to the hospital, to work at the day care, to class…wherever. Instead, she allowed herself to enjoy the fragrant warmth of the water for as long as she wanted—a luxury of time Jake had provided. Her eyes flew open at the thought. Bringing Mae here helped Joanna as much as it helped Mae. Jake had known that. How was she supposed to stop caring about a man like that?

Jake had a briefcase in his hand, and his head was down when he entered the house many hours later. He seemed unaware of Joanna's presence as she sat silently in the chair in the corner of the darkened living room.

"Hello, Jake," she said softly, but if he was surprised, he did not show it.

The corners of his mouth lifted in a generous smile

as he studied her for a moment before answering. "I didn't think you'd still be awake. It's after midnight." He loosened his necktie before dropping his briefcase and jacket into a nearby chair.

"I wanted to see you before I went to sleep." Her voice wavered, and she paused for a moment. "I want to thank you."

He tilted his head in unspoken question as he approached her.

"I mean, for bringing Mae here, for my plane ticket, for hiring Ina to stay here. For all the inconvenience you're willing to put up with to help Aunt Mae, to help me. I think it's rather noble of you."

"Noble?" His laugh was gentle. "I doubt that's the right word, but thank you for the thought."

"And the bedroom, it's beautiful but unnecessary."

"It needed to be remodeled," he said. "This seemed liked a good time to take care of it."

"And the paintings, Jake...they're lovely."

He nodded with a hint of satisfaction tugging at one corner of his mouth. "I bought those a long time ago." They reminded me of you, he almost added, but decided it was better left unsaid. He slid a hand into his pocket and looked down at the carpet for a moment trying to sort out what he was feeling from what he could say. "Ina selected most of the furnishings. I asked her to make your room resemble one you'd find if you could see into a window of one of those English cottages."

Joanna swallowed at the lump that rose in her

throat. "And...it does...." An instant of pain squeezed her heart.

Jake was standing beside her now, and Joanna had to tilt her head back slightly to look up at him. Her heart pounded mercilessly within her. She'd come here to get over this man, she reminded herself. Not to fall hopelessly in love with him.

Jake knew they needed a change of conversation before nostalgia overtook their emotions. "I apologize for not picking you up at the airport this afternoon, Jo. I'd intended to be there."

"It's all right. Ina told me you were delayed at the hospital."

"Yes," he replied. "You'll see that the cancellation of personal plans is a frequent and unfortunate consequence of being in the medical profession." His mouth slanted into a smile that softened the negative quality of his comment.

Joanna smiled back. "I had a chance to get acquainted with Ina. She's a sweet lady."

"I knew you'd like her." Jake placed a hand against the back of the chair as he studied the dark eyes that viewed him—gentle eyes he'd never forget, not even when Joanna was gone.

Joanna shifted nervously in her seat when Jake's silence prolonged the awkward moment. "I—I'm glad Ina's here, but I'm sorry that you had to go to the expense of hiring live-in help because of me."

Jake gave a dismissive shrug. "It's no problem. Ina already works here on a part-time basis. Turning this into a live-in position temporarily was a simple matter, and I think she likes it."

"But the costs—"

"Don't worry about it," Jake told her. "Ina will help you settle in. She attends services at a church just up the road a few miles. I'm sure she'd like it if you went with her while you're here. She already has plans to involve you in a children's Sunday school class."

"She didn't mention that to me. I'll have to ask her about it," Joanna responded as she rose from the living room chair and smoothed the folds from her plum-colored sweater.

"I doubt you'll need to ask Ina very many questions. You'll find she volunteers information quite freely," Jake said, his smile widening.

Joanna gave a soft laugh. "Ina does seem to enjoy talking."

"Yes, she does," he agreed. "Did she give you the credit cards?"

"Yes, but I don't want them, Jake. You've paid for my ticket, my coat and boots, and you're letting me stay here to be with Aunt Mae. I want to be able to pay you back and you've done so much already—"

"No arguments, Jo." He cut off her protest as they walked together toward the staircase. "Buy whatever you need. I trust your judgment."

"But the car, Jake. Ina gave me the keys to that blue car and told me it's mine to use while I'm here. I can't accept that."

"It's a rental. When you leave, I'll send it back. You'll need transportation while you're here and, in case you haven't noticed, there aren't any bus stops out here in the country."

"I'm going to find some temporary work while I'm here so I can repay at least part of the money." Joanna stood at the foot of the stairs, looking up into smoky gray eyes that showed no hint of the answers she was seeking.

"There's no need. Don't worry about it," Jake assured her before an uncomfortable stillness fell between them.

"Aunt Mae seemed to be doing very well today," Joanna said. "She's better than she was in the hospital."

"Yes," he agreed. "The cardiologist saw her yesterday. He changed her medication. He will come by the house tomorrow to check on her."

"I think you may have saved her life by bringing her here," Joanna admitted the thought that had awed her. How much Jake had been willing to give up to help Mae.

"I want her to have the best chance she can." Jake rubbed a hand against the muscles in the back of his neck. "Did Mae ever tell you how much she loves Indiana farmland?" he asked, with a gentle laugh. "Years ago she told me stories about growing up around here. I think that's why she liked me so much that first time we met at the clinic. She found out I was from this part of the country, and that was all it took."

Joanna's laugh was soft. "No, she'd have loved you even if you were city born and bred. You're the son she always wanted and never had."

"Maybe," Jake replied, "But either way, I'm grateful. She's a pleasure to know."

"Yes, she is," she agreed before another awkward silence had to be chased away. "You have a beautiful home, Jake. Ina showed me around."

"It was my father's." His words were suddenly quiet, solemn. The house had belonged to his mother, too, for a few years. Before she'd walked out on them. But he wouldn't acknowledge it. Not to Joanna, barely even to himself. He could hardly remember the woman whose absence had left more of an imprint on his life than her brief presence ever did. But that was enough reflection on unpleasant memories for one night. What had they been discussing? The house, he recalled. "This place is pretty much the way my father left it." Except for Joanna's room.

"It's very...picturesque," she replied, and he looked away from her, down to the dark wood of the banister. She stopped talking, sensing his mood change. Had she managed to say something wrong already? During their first conversation? "I—I appreciate everything you're doing for Aunt Mae and for me," she offered in a gentle voice.

Jake met her gaze, his eyes guarded again. Unreadable. "I know," he replied. "But you'll need to rely on Ina, not me. I'm not going to be here much." He'd make sure of it. He'd decided that the moment he'd asked her to come.

Joanna nodded her head. "I'll sit with Aunt Mae as much as I can so you can cut down on the expense of hired help."

"That's not necessary. There's a steady stream of caretakers in and out of here," he answered. "Mae just needs you around for moral support, I think. And comfort. I realize you two are very close.''

"She's been good to me," Joanna responded, placing her hands on the smooth wood railing. "She accepted me as family from the moment we met. Unconditional love. After my difficult childhood years, I needed that.''

Jake gave a brief nod, not trusting himself to speak. The subject of her troubled past was not a good one to embark on. It brought too many painful emotions to the forefront that he wasn't capable of dealing with tonight. It would make Joanna sad, and he couldn't bear to see her sad again. Even if it wasn't his fault, this time.

"Well…" she began hesitantly, "I guess I'll say good night.''

"Good night, Jo," Jake responded as he watched her turn and make her way up the staircase to the second story of this house. His house. In the two years he'd lived here alone, he couldn't count the times he'd wondered how it would be to have her here, in his home, with him. Now, here she was, against his better judgment. And on this first night, it was proving to be as impossible as he'd suspected it would be. Jake shook his head in a mixture of frustration and sadness. There could be no future for them together; nothing had happened to change that. Now, all he had to do was stop wanting it…wanting her.

Chapter Three

"We could use you for however many weeks you're available, Miss Meccord. Could you start tomorrow?" the administrator of Smithfield Children's Home asked at the end of an extensive interview.

"Yes, definitely," Joanna replied. "I certainly can."

"Fine. Come in around four o'clock so you can have dinner with us and meet the children."

Joanna had the urge to hug the man, but he looked so dignified sitting behind his large oak desk, she decided against it. "Yes, I'll be here. Thank you, sir."

"Glad to have you on board." The gray-haired gentleman stood up, extending a hand to Joanna. "We'll be expecting you tomorrow."

"Yes, sir. Thank you." Joanna shook his hand before finding her way to the personnel office where she picked up the necessary forms. Then she headed for her rental car. A part-time temporary job. She couldn't wait to share the news with Ina, and thank her for her help in getting this position.

Pulling into the driveway, Joanna saw Jake's silver sports car parked next to the garage. She gathered up the paperwork, slid her purse over her shoulder and hurried through the crisp wintry air toward the house. She pushed open the front door and stepped into a hallway filled with the aroma of a bakery. It smelled wonderful. Like home. Except, not any home Joanna could actually remember.

"Ina?"

"In the kitchen, dear," Ina called from the far end of the house.

Dropping her car keys into her small handbag, Joanna hung her coat in the closet and headed toward the kitchen. "Hi!"

"Hello," they greeted her. Jake sat at the table with a half-eaten slice of peach pie in front of him and the morning newspaper in his hands.

"Want a piece of pie?" Ina asked. "Freshly baked."

"Not right now, but thanks. It looks delicious," Joanna responded. She glanced toward Jake and was surprised to see him wearing a casual navy shirt and jeans. And glasses. "I've never seen you wear glasses," she commented. She liked the look.

"That's because we haven't been around each other much for the past two years," he replied as he looked up from his paper.

"How did your interview go?" Ina asked, wiping her hands on a dishtowel.

"Great!" Joanna exclaimed. "I got the job!"

Ina opened her arms, enveloping Joanna in a big hug. "That's wonderful, dear. I'm so happy for you!"

"What job?" Jake asked with obvious surprise. "You haven't been here more than forty-eight hours."

"I know, but Ina told me about Smithfield Children's Home. She knows several people who work there, and she made a few calls. They needed some temporary help to work with the children...someone with a social work background. And I got the job! I can't wait to tell Aunt Mae."

But the idea didn't seem to please Jake. "You don't need a job while you're here, Joanna. If you need more money—"

"I don't want to ask for money, Jake. I'd like to be able to even pay you back for some of what you're doing."

"It's not necessary. Don't feel that you need to do that."

Joanna smiled and gave an uncertain shrug. "I may not be able to do that even with this job. It doesn't exactly pay well. Is there any iced tea, Ina?"

"In the refrigerator, dear," Ina answered.

"Thanks," Joanna replied and opened the door. Lifting the pitcher from the top shelf, she poured some of the drink into a tall glass. "But it will be wonderful experience for me working with the kids. Do you want some tea?"

"No, thanks," Jake responded.

"Don't you want to join us, Ina?" Joanna asked when she noticed Ina had returned to the kitchen sink to finish rinsing some dishes.

"No, thank you. You go ahead," Ina said, glancing over her shoulder.

"Smithfield Children's Home," Jake repeated and sent an inquiring look with a sharp lift of his brows in Ina's direction.

Joanna noticed the exchange. "Yes. They have about a hundred kids there, Jake. Boys and girls, all ages. They're children going through transitional periods in their lives—moving from one foster home to another or out of a treatment center into an adoptive placement." She spoke in such a rush of words, she had to pause for a quick breath, which brought a grin from Jake. "It's a wonderful place!" she added with enthusiasm.

"Yes, it is," he agreed with a nod. "I thought so myself the first time I visited it."

"You've been there?" Joanna sat down.

"I'm there every Wednesday morning for an hour or two. When do you start?" Jake asked before taking another bite of pie.

"Tomorrow. But, what do you mean you're there every Wednesday? What do you do there?"

"The same things I do daily at my office," he replied. "I see patients who are sick or injured. The kids, I mean."

"But..." She glanced over at Ina who was busy concentrating on the dishes in the sink rather than facing Joanna just then. "Ina, you didn't tell me Jake was one of the people who worked there."

"Didn't I mention that?" Ina responded without looking up. "I meant to."

Sure you did, Joanna thought. How convenient for

Ina to forget that one piece of information. Joanna returned her gaze to the man seated beside her at the table. "Should I thank you for getting this job for me?"

"No, not at all," Jake assured. "I didn't know anything about this, and I'm not in favor of you working right now. Especially not at Smithfield. Putting yourself in a setting like that with all those troubled kids...it won't be easy for you, Joanna. It will bring back bad memories of your own childhood." He paused. "Are you sure you're prepared for that?"

"I have to be. Social work is what I want to do. Being an advocate for those children is my career goal. I can't help them if I'm not exposed to them, can I?" she explained, defending her choices.

Jake wasn't pleased. She could see it in that shadowy frown that hovered at the corners of his mouth. But she could be just as determined as he could, Joanna assured herself and gave a slight but definite lift of her chin.

Jake's tight expression relaxed into a smile before he looked down briefly at the plate and fork on the table. "It's your decision," he commented. When he raised his gaze to meet hers again, all humor was gone. "Just be careful. I don't want you to get hurt. Mae's health is enough of a concern without having your heart broken over some child you can't help."

It might be easier to deal with than some other forms of heartbreak, Joanna longed to reply. But she didn't. She simply nodded in silence and then turned to Ina. "Are we going tonight?"

"Yes," Ina said. "Be ready by six-forty-five."

"What do you two have planned?" Jake asked.

"Bible study," Joanna replied. "Ina says they're studying the book of Ephesians."

"Ephesians," Jake repeated as Ina quietly slipped from the room.

"Yes. They're studying about the Lord's love for us and our spiritual riches in Christ," Joanna explained, then noticed how closely Jake was studying her as she spoke. "You know…about how God gave his Son so we could be forgiven for our sins." She knew that Jake was familiar with some of what she was talking about. They'd discussed it before. Several times.

"You really believe all of that, don't you? That people must find some sort of a personal relationship with God?" Jake's questions were straightforward and serious, not belittling in the least.

"Absolutely."

"There are a lot of people in the world—good people—who wouldn't agree with you."

"No one is saved by being a good person. It's more than that. Salvation is a gift from God," Joanna explained. "It's never a matter of just doing enough good deeds, Jake. There are two completely different roads in life—the Lord's way or the way of the world. Everyone has a time in their life when they're standing at the crossroads and has to make a decision." She wondered if she should invite him to join them. It was worth a try. "If you'd like, you could come with us tonight. The pastor could do a much better job of explaining these things to you than I can."

But Jake shook his head. "Thanks, but I can't tonight, Jo. I'm meeting Daniel Vernon at the gym to play basketball. He's one of Andrew's sons."

Joanna smiled. "I remember you mentioning him before. You went to school with Daniel, didn't you?"

"Yes," Jake answered. "Sorry about tonight. Maybe some other time?"

"Sure. Some other time," she agreed, wondering if such a time would come. And when. "I'll see you later." She turned to go just as Jake stood up.

"Joanna…" he called after her.

She looked back.

"How did it feel when you stood at those crossroads?"

Joanna had to stop and really think for a moment. It had been so long ago. "I think I felt…loved. Loved by God in a way I'd never been loved by anyone else."

"Like God Himself stood there? Waiting?" he asked.

"Yes," she agreed quickly, surprised by his insight. "But there was no thunder or lightning. No messenger angel. Just a still, small voice inside me." She raised a hand to her heart. "In here."

Jake's eyes followed the movement of her hand before returning to lock with her gaze. There was something there, some sadness, something complex Joanna couldn't identify. Something she couldn't help him with. Every ounce of her wanted to make right whatever was so wrong within him, but it wasn't her wrong to right. "The Lord only wants us to love Him, Jake."

A look of utter weariness crossed Jake's face before he glanced up at the clock. "I've got to get go-ing. We'll have to talk another time."

She nodded but worried about the strained tone of his voice. "I—I'll go upstairs to sit with Aunt Mae. She seemed to be feeling better this morning."

Jake agreed. "She's hanging in there. I was with her earlier, and we talked quite a bit."

About what, Joanna wondered. Spiritual matters, maybe? Not knowing what else to do, Joanna excused herself and headed toward the staircase. She'd been a Christian since she was twelve years old, many years before she moved in with her aunt. Why, after all these years, did talking about her faith seem like such a private matter? Why was it still so difficult to dis-cuss with Jake? Maybe because she cared so much about his reaction? Because those people dearest to the heart are the ones who seem slowest to accept the truth? Hadn't Aunt Mae warned her about that a long time ago?

After her parents' deaths, Joanna had spent her childhood years with no connection to her past. Her adoptive parents had not allowed her access to avail-able information. When she'd turned eighteen, she'd begun searching for any relatives she might have left from her biological family. That's when she'd dis-covered she had a widowed aunt, and Aunt Mae had been delighted to meet the niece she'd prayed for over the years. The Lord had led Joanna home to the roots she'd been hoping for. An aunt with a heart full of love. That was tangible evidence to Joanna of what God could do. She wished there was some evidence she could produce for Jake to help him believe.

A gush of frigid air literally pushed Joanna and Ina inside the front door as they returned from church services that evening.

"Jake won't be home until late," Ina said after she'd listened to the messages on the answering machine. "He was called to the hospital because Andrew needed him."

Joanna placed her coat along with Ina's in the hallway closet. "But Jake was supposed to go to the gym for a while. Does Dr. Vernon usually call him for help?"

"Andrew Vernon is nearly ready to retire, and, if you ask me, he depends on Dr. Barnes too much. Things will be easier when Andrew retires and a younger doctor comes in to help out." Ina walked toward the stairs, but not without stopping beside Joanna to give an affectionate pat on her arm. "I'll see you in the morning, dear. I'm going to check in on Mae and the nurse, then go on to bed."

"Okay," Joanna said with a smile. "I'll say goodnight to Aunt Mae, too. Then I think I'll sit down here for a while and read. See you in the morning."

After finding Mae sleeping peacefully for the night, Joanna went back downstairs. Curling up in the large comfortable chair in the corner of the living room, she read one of Ina's magazines until she grew sleepy. Then she switched off the light and leaned her head against the wing of the chair.

A warm hand squeezed her shoulder gently, and Joanna stirred in the chair. Her drowsy eyes opened slowly to find Jake standing beside her in the living room.

"Hi, sleepyhead," he said quietly, but when Joanna met his gaze, she saw a gloominess there she'd not seen before. Not that she could ever recall. He looked tired, but it was much more than that. It was sorrow. Stark and real. She sat up suddenly.

"Jake, what's wrong? Is it Aunt Mae?" she asked in a voice still raspy with sleep.

"Mae's fine. Don't be frightened," he assured her and for the first time since she'd awakened, he looked away.

"But something's wrong," she persisted. Glancing up at the lighted grandfather clock in the corner of the room, she saw that it was nearly one o'clock in the morning. "You've been at the hospital? All this time?"

"Yes," he said in the hush of the room. Only the ticking of the clock broke the silence.

Joanna moved out of the chair and onto the ottoman. She patted her hand against the cushion, still warm from the presence of her body. "Sit down. Tell me what's happened," she urged softly.

Jake sat down, sinking into the comfort of the over-stuffed chair.

"What is it?" she whispered.

"One of Andrew's patients died tonight. Mr. Littner. He was an elderly gentleman. I didn't really know the man, but I've never seen Andrew take anything so hard."

"Was it sudden? Unexpected?"

Jake didn't answer immediately but ran a hand

wearily over his eyes. "He'd been ill for several months so it wasn't totally unexpected, but Andrew was surprised that it happened this soon. This quickly." He looked at Joanna. "Mr. Littner gave up. Simply gave up. And died."

She touched Jake's arm, waiting for him to continue.

"He said he was ready to go…that there wasn't anything left on this earth worth living for."

"Didn't he have a family?" Joanna asked.

"His wife died about a year ago, and he lost his only daughter when she was a child. He didn't want to live, Jo. He said he was ready to go home to be with his Lord."

"Then he's better off now than he was here on this Earth, sickly and with no loved ones."

"Can it be like that?" Jake's eyes were bleak, desolate. "Can you be certain that what you believe is the truth?"

"Yes," she answered, nodding her head. "I'm certain, Jake, with all my heart. But I had to trust God…to really completely trust Him." Trust. She wondered if that was the stumbling block. Did Jake trust anyone? Completely?

He sat very still, looking so intently at Joanna she wondered if he could somehow see into her soul.

"Let me get my Bible," she began, "and I can show you some verses—"

"No, please," Jake said, cutting off her words and stinging her with his sudden disinterest. "It's late. We're both tired."

But Joanna realized that the late hour was only an

excuse. Opening a Bible and finding the right verses might force Jake to face the decision he wasn't ready to make. She stood up and gave what she hoped was an understanding smile. "Maybe some other time then. I'm sorry about Mr. Littner. And Andrew."

Jake gave a distracted nod in a gesture of thanks before Joanna turned to leave.

"Good night," she said. Then she disappeared up the stairs. And Jake watched her go.

When Joanna reached the second floor, she went directly to Mae's room where she checked on her aunt and said good-night to the nurse who was seated next to the bedside engrossed in a thick novel. Then Joanna headed for her own room. She changed out of her jeans and sweater and into a thin nightgown that was designed more for South Carolina's nights than Indiana's. But, nestling down into the bed, she warmed up quickly despite her inability to sleep. Her first day on a new job started in several hours, but she wasn't worried. It felt right and she knew how to work with the children. No, it was Jake that worried her. She used to think of herself as being alone. But she didn't feel so alone anymore. Not since Aunt Mae had come into her life. Then Jake, and now Ina. This time it was Jake who seemed alone. And there had to be moments, like tonight, when he felt it. She'd been there when he'd come home, she realized, but only in a distant kind of way. Why couldn't she be the comfort to him that he'd been to her in days gone by? Then her mind went back to the evening they'd lost all that, and more.

Joanna's twentieth birthday. Mae had planned a

special dinner at Joanna's favorite restaurant, but when the time came to go, Mae wasn't feeling well. Rather than cancel the reservations and spoil the occasion, Jake had suggested that he and Joanna go by themselves. They hadn't seen each other much over the past few weeks, and it would be a chance for them to talk. And he wanted her birthday to be a special one,

So they went to the restaurant Mae had selected, which sat atop the highest hotel in the city. And it was wonderful—the food, the sights. The company. Joanna couldn't remember a better evening in all her life, and it passed all too quickly....

They were among the last customers to leave the restaurant that night, and their conversation didn't lag on the long drive home. It was only when Jake pulled his car into Mae's driveway that an awkward silence fell between them. The engine off, the lights out. Only the dim porch lamp offered relief from the darkness of the night.

"Thank you for a perfect evening, Jake." She shifted in her seat to look into his unfathomable eyes. Had he enjoyed their time together, too? He'd certainly been attentive the past few hours. He'd sat across the table from her, talking, laughing, looking at her, she suspected, in some new way. More like the young woman she was and not the teenager she had been when they'd first met. If his goal on this night of her birthday was to make her feel like the most important woman in the world, he'd more than succeeded. She felt like the most important woman in

his world. It had been a lovely feeling but, she knew, it was time for it to end.

Jake reached for her hand and slowly pressed her fingers to his mouth for a kiss. Her hand was soft, sweet. Free of any rings of belonging to another. "It's been special for me, too," he admitted as he battled an unexpected desire. He wanted her closer. Next to him. In his arms.

Jake cleared his throat quietly and lowered their hands to the seat but couldn't quite let go. He laced his fingers through hers.

"Yes, very special," Joanna agreed. She straightened and sighed softly, knowing it was getting late. "I guess it's time to say good-night." No matter how much she didn't want to. She glanced down at their interlocking fingers, then back into his gaze. His eyes held hers and suddenly she knew. He felt it, too. Perhaps as strongly as she did.

Jake nodded but didn't speak. He couldn't think of a response. At the moment, all he could think of was Joanna and how beautiful she was. Absolutely beautiful—in looks and in spirit. He'd never been as acutely aware of that fact as he was tonight. It knifed through him in a way it never had.

"Joanna..." he whispered as his hands moved to touch her satin-smooth face. Then his hands slid into her soft, loose hair, pulling her easily into a gentle kiss that slowly grew as needy as either had ever known. The warmth of Jake's mouth over hers felt like the most natural thing in the world to Joanna. She wondered how she'd lived this long without it. When Jake touched her shoulders, bringing her

closer, she slowly, instinctively slid her arms around his neck, deepening his response and clouding her thoughts. Never had anything felt so right. She wanted more. Of him, of them, of whatever it was they were finding here together tonight. Her fingers wandered into his dark, silky hair.

"Joanna..." he murmured her name again. His breath flowed warmly along the delicate line of her throat. Her soft sigh in reply did nothing to discourage him when his mouth trailed light, tiny kisses down her neck to a smooth shoulder covered with only a thin strap of a summer dress. Jake felt her sharp intake of breath at the contact. He hesitated, his lips lingering intimately against the curve of her shoulder as he tried to reason with himself. This was Joanna in his arms. His friend. And he wanted her more at that moment than he'd ever wanted anyone in his life. His entire life. And it was crazy. She was sweet, innocent...and young. Too young. Jake stopped—instantly—and lifted his head to look into her barely open eyes. What were they doing? What was he doing? "Joanna...this is crazy," he barely breathed the words before he pulled away from her completely, raising a hand to his mouth.

"Jake?" she whispered in the stillness. Free of his touch, she'd never felt colder in all her life.

"I'm sorry," he answered in a voice deadly quiet with realization.

"But—"

Jake's words brought her questions to a halt. "I care about you, Jo, very much, but this..."

"What's wrong?" she asked despite the uneasiness

*settling over her at the distance in the voice that had
murmured her name with such longing only moments
earlier. "What did I do—"*

*"Nothing," he assured her before rubbing his hand
down his face. He leaned back against the seat being
careful not to touch her as he did so. "It's what I'm
doing that's the problem."*

*Stung but confused, she watched him close his eyes
in disgust, frustration...something she couldn't identify. "Jake...we're not doing anything—"*

*"We're not doing anything," he repeated in dis-
belief. "Do you kiss every man you go out with like
that?" The question was blunt. Angry.*

*"No! Of course, I don't," she replied. "I've never
kissed anyone...like that. How could you ask?"*

*"Because we were doing plenty, Joanna, whether
you realize it or not. And we're headed toward much
more."*

*Her face flushed with humiliation. Were they? Was
she being careless? She'd never been in a situation
quite like this, and it had been difficult to think when
Jake was holding her.*

*"You should go inside," he stated. The look of con-
cern in his eyes only made her feel worse. "C'mon.
I'll walk you to the door."*

"But I don't want to go in yet."

*"And I don't want you to, either. That's exactly
why you have to go now." He reached for the car
door.*

"But, Jake—"

*"Don't you see?" he asked urgently, ending her
protest. "We can want each other, we can have each*

other…but it won't lead to a future together. And that's what you'll need."

Joanna felt chilled. She looked down at her hands, which were now folded neatly together in her lap. Jake didn't want her, wouldn't want her—not for anything more than this? She could hardly believe his warning. "We've known each other a long time, Jake. I thought we were friends—"

"We are friends," he insisted before reaching out to touch her hair. The softness was almost unbearable and he pulled his hand away. "I don't ever want to lose that. And, we will…if we let this happen."

"You can't know that—"

"I do know. You have no idea how complicated things can get." Jake exhaled a heavy sigh. She had no idea how uncomplicated he wanted things to remain. Joanna was a woman he would chose neither to hurt nor to have. He'd seen what a love like this could do to a person, what it had done to his own father, and he wanted no part in it. But how was he supposed to explain that to her? To this tenderhearted young woman he could too easily love? "Jo, listen to me," Jake began as he reached to touch her hand.

But Joanna pulled away. She sat only a few inches from him, her arms crossed in front of her. "It's Dr. Eden, isn't it? Natalie Eden?" she asked.

Jake hesitated. She didn't know how little he'd ever allowed anyone to mean to him. Including Dr. Eden. She didn't know he wanted it that way, kept it that way. Intentionally. And he wasn't going to tell Joanna that now. He breathed an undistinguishable curse under his breath. This was his fault, and he should have *known better than to let it happen. Joanna was still practically a kid. How could he have allowed things to get so mixed-up? How could he undo this mess? No way, he knew. None. Unless he lied.*

"Is it because of Dr. Eden?" Joanna repeated, her heart near to breaking.

"Natalie and I have known each other for a long time..." Jake said and stopped. Being dishonest with Joanna was something he could hardly make himself do. Maybe if he just stopped there, didn't say anything more... Maybe, he hoped, the implication would be enough. And it was.

"I understand," Joanna replied in a voice barely audible.

She watched the line of his mouth tighten but had no idea that it was all Jake could do to refrain from telling her that, no, she didn't understand. She couldn't understand how close he found himself to loving her—Joanna Meccord. Not Dr. Eden or any other woman he'd known. And the thought unnerved him. It was his deep affection for this unassuming young woman that had blindsided him this evening. He'd known her for so long, liked her so much, he hadn't seen this coming. It simply hadn't occurred to him to put up defenses to something he'd never imagined existed. Not with Joanna.

Their walk to the front door that evening was a silent one with Jake regretting his actions while Joanna wondered if all hope was lost for them. Jake wasn't going to give them this chance they'd stumbled upon. Joanna sensed it, felt it...even more than his words had proclaimed it. He was sorry for this eve-

ning's events. He'd undo all of it if he could, and that thought cut through the heart she'd just discovered could belong to him, if only he wanted it.

They walked up onto the porch and approached the front door. It was time for the inevitable goodbye. But Jake owed her more than goodbye. "Joanna..." he began. "I care about you...very much...more than you know."

Joanna's eyes misted with wistful thoughts of what might have been. "I understand. You don't have to say anything more. You need someone like Natalie Eden. A doctor, a professional woman nearer your own age and position in life. I know I'm not right for you." She watched his mouth dip into a deep frown.

"Jo, you're a beautiful woman, a wonderful friend, but—"

"Good night, Jake," she interrupted. She didn't want to hear platitudes and apologies. Joanna reached for the door, but Jake quickly covered her hand with his own.

"There's nothing we can do to change what's happened," he admitted, "and there's no way we can forget. I'm not sure either of us would really want to."

She turned her head to meet his gaze and was surprised by the glimpse of misery she found there. "Then, why...?"

"Why can't we be together?" Jake finished her thought for her. "We just can't. I don't want the kind of life you're going to need. I can't give you that." He hesitated. "Find someone who will, Jo. I want you to be happy."

"But," Joanna began, *"you make me happy. I don't need a guarantee of what the future holds. I— I just need you."*

He'd never felt like a bigger louse in all his thirty-two years. How had he let her come to need him? She'd been a contented friend a few hours ago until he opened up possibilities and emotions between them that shouldn't exist.

"Please, don't need me," he replied as gently as he could. *"Believe me when I tell you it wouldn't work. I'm truly sorry."* Jake leaned forward, pressing his mouth against her forehead in a light, but lingering kiss.

They parted that night with an awkwardness they'd not known before and successfully avoided each other for the next several days. Then one day while Joanna was working at the day care center, Jake came.

It was a damp day in late winter, but many of the teachers had brought their students outside to the playground for the afternoon. Mrs. Clark, the teacher of the class with which Joanna helped, was no exception.

"The children are being so good today," Joanna said, glancing up from the tiny, raven-haired youngster she was pushing in a swing.

"Hmm…" Mrs. Clark was obviously not listening as she looked out past Joanna toward the fence. *"I'm wondering who your young admirer is."*

"With all the people on this playground, what makes you think it's me someone is admiring?" Joanna laughed, but curious at the comment, she looked in the direction Mrs. Clark had been staring.

Her heart skipped a beat. There was a long distance between them, too much to be certain, but somehow she knew it was Jake.

"Well, was I right?" Mrs. Clark asked. "Do you know him?"

"It's Jake," she responded and raised a hand to protect her eyes from the sun. "Jake Barnes."

A gracious smile warmed Mrs. Clark's face. "The young doctor you've spoken of?"

"Yes," Joanna replied. "The one who's dating someone else."

"Well, he's not here looking at that someone else now, is he? Why don't you go talk to him?"

Joanna hesitated as she surveyed the activity on the playground. "But the children—"

"The children will be fine, and I can watch them for myself for a few minutes. Now, take a break and go say hello to that young man over there before I do," Mrs. Clark protested successfully.

Sliding one hand into the deep pocket of her colorful work smock, she began crossing the grassy area of the park. In an attempt to push the windblown strands from her face, she ran slender fingers through her ash-blond hair. She had not seen Jake for days. Not since her birthday. And whatever composure she could manage in his presence would be fragile at best. Unsure what to expect, she took a deep breath and approached him.

"Hello," she offered, attempting to sound casual while her heart pounded so loudly in her ears, she feared she would not hear his reply.

"Hello," he answered and nodded toward the busy playground. "I'm glad you could get away."

"I only have a couple of minutes." As she spoke, Joanna managed to lower her gaze from his to focus on the collar of his shirt. Hugging her arms to her stomach, she fought the chill running through her. If he were only to touch her, she knew she would feel warm again.

And Jake reached out, brushing warm fingers against her cheek. He'd witnessed many painful scenes in his life, but never one quite like this. He'd seen the hurt in her wary eyes, hurt he knew he was responsible for. But this was a personal pain, too. Self-inflicted. "We need to talk."

Joanna squinted, holding hot tears in check. Unable to speak without emotion, she simply nodded her head in agreement.

Jake watched her lower her gaze to the grass at her feet rather than meet his eyes, and he was grateful. He wasn't sure he could say the words if she looked him in the eyes. "I came here to tell you something before you hear it from someone else."

Joanna glanced up. It couldn't be good.

"I'm going away, Jo. Back home."

"Not now." The words escaped before Joanna could stop them.

"Yes, now," he replied firmly. "I'm going back home to Indiana to take over my father's private practice."

"But, Jake…" she began. Didn't he have any of the same mixed-up feelings for her that she had for *him? How could he walk away like this? "That's so far away."*

"I know, but it's my home. It's where I belong."

A rush of tears flooded Joanna's eyes, and she looked away, not understanding what was happening to her. She'd spent a lifetime of moving here and there throughout her childhood. Losing friends, finding new ones—it had been a way of life. But, with Jake... Why was her heart breaking now? How could one night change everything?

"Don't cry," Jake said quietly, his mouth tight and grim. Placing a hand under her chin, he tilted her head up gently and forced her to meet his gaze. "Don't waste your tears or your dreams on me, Jo."

And with those words, he'd walked out of her life.

Joanna's bittersweet memories of days gone by brought fresh tears to the surface, but she brushed them away. She had more to worry about than the fact that Jake Barnes didn't love her. There were other harsh realities of life to be dealt with.

Wrapping a pillow around the back of her head, she closed her eyes to whisper her prayers. She reminded the Lord of the weather forecast for tomorrow, as if He didn't already know. Ten to twelve inches of snow. Her first day of work, and she'd rarely driven on icy roads. She definitely had more to be concerned about than a future without Jake Barnes. She had to get through tomorrow.

Chapter Four

The door to the car flew open, and biting air crashed over Joanna.

"Are you crazy?" Jake's voice boomed over the roar of the wind. "What are you trying to do? Kill yourself?" He gripped her forearm, pulling her from the stalled vehicle.

Joanna stepped out into a snowdrift that was deeper than the top of her boots. Snow slid down inside the lining. "I'm freezing...." She rubbed her hands together, trying to rid herself of the numbness. "Thank God, you found me."

"Yes, do thank God because He's the *only* reason I found you. I could barely see your car down in this ditch from the road." He put his arm around her shoulders for support. "Are you all right?"

"Yes. I haven't been out here very long."

"It doesn't take long to freeze to death in this kind of weather, Joanna," he responded sharply. "We've got to get home."

"But the car..." She glanced over her shoulder at the stranded vehicle.

"We'll take care of it tomorrow. Let's go," he ordered.

The wind howled around her ears, and she gripped Jake's arm tightly as they began climbing the embankment. Trudging through the snow, every step felt heavier than the one before it. The incline was only several feet high but very steep, and it loomed like a mountain before Joanna's eyes. Gusts of frigid air whipped her face so that she could scarcely catch her breath, and she put her gloved hand over her mouth.

At the top of the embankment, Jake stepped up onto the icy road and hauled Joanna up out of the snow. She lost her footing when her boot hit the slick pavement, and she fell against him. Reaching for the side of his car, Jake braced them from the fall as another fierce arctic blast rocked them.

Jake pulled open the driver's door, shouting over the raging wind. "Get in! Hurry up!"

Joanna crawled into the small car, over the gearshift and onto the passenger seat. Her nearly frozen limbs restricted her to slow, awkward movements. Immediately, Jake climbed in behind the steering wheel and slammed the door to cut off the bone-chilling air. The motor was still running and the warmth from the heater filled the automobile, stinging Joanna's fingertips.

"Give me your hands," he instructed, and she removed the soggy gloves, letting them fall onto the floorboard. Taking her hands in his, he rubbed them briskly. Jake raised them to his mouth to blow warm breath over them, and the friction gradually caused more feeling to return to Joanna's fingers.

"Better?"

"It hurts," she replied.

"It will stop eventually. What in the world were you doing out in this storm?"

"Going to work," she responded hesitantly and pulled her hands away from him.

"To work? I could have told you the only place you were going was right into the nearest ditch."

"But this is my first day, Jake. If I don't show up, I might lose this job."

"Then lose it. No one can go anywhere in weather like this." He turned on the windshield wipers and edged his car from the side of the road. "You've probably never driven on roads this icy before today. How could you expect to drive in an actual blizzard?"

"The weather wasn't this bad when I started out. All of this wind and blowing snow...it came out of nowhere," she explained.

Feeling the car slide beneath them, Joanna stared ahead into the swirling whiteness. The storm had gained intensity even in the last few minutes. "How can you see where we're going?"

"I can't," he admitted, "But we can't stay here, so I'm going to attempt to get us home."

The car slid several feet to the side, and Jake again guided it back toward the center of the road. "This would be a good time to put one of those prayers of yours to work."

She glanced at him to find a stern look on his face

and his steady grip on the steering wheel as he stared straight ahead.

"I'm not kidding, Jo," he replied to her questioning look. "We'll be lucky if we don't end up in another ditch...or worse."

Joanna knew luck would have nothing to do with it, so pray is exactly what she did as they forged slowly homeward. Her silent prayers did not stop until they pulled safely into the driveway nearly an hour later.

"I'm tracking water all over the carpet," Joanna said as they came through the front door. She sat down on the steps leading upstairs and began tugging unsuccessfully at one of her boots.

"Here," Jake said as he bent down. "I'll get it." He removed both of her boots easily, exposing bright robin's-egg-blue socks, soaked from melted snow. He grinned.

"I like colorful things," Joanna defended with a shrug of embarrassment as she began peeling the socks from her wet feet.

"Obviously," Jake replied, his smile widening. Then he disappeared into the kitchen, returning momentarily with several small towels.

He pulled the cap from her head and placed it with their coats as Joanna rubbed her damp hair briskly with one of the towels he handed to her.

"Your hair is wet, too, Jake. You didn't even have a hat on out there."

He ignored her comment. "You had no business going out in this blizzard."

"I know that now. I tried to turn around when I

saw that the storm was getting worse, but that's when I slid off the road. I didn't realize—"

"Now, you *do* realize how dangerous that was. You've got to be more careful."

"I will from now on. I promise. Thank you for coming after me. It was foolish, I know, but the most important thing at the time seemed to be getting to work," she admitted halfheartedly.

"Not important enough to risk your life. Few things are." A frown creased his forehead. "What you really need is to get out of those wet clothes and into a hot bath. But the electricity is off so the pump on the well isn't working. That translates into no water. Hot or otherwise."

Joanna looked away from his steady gaze with obvious effort. "I—I should call Smithfield to let them know I won't be coming in."

"No calls tonight, Jo. In or out. The phone lines are down, too."

Joanna rubbed the towel lightly against her hair, and she stood up. "I guess I may as well change. Is anyone with Aunt Mae?"

"Yes," Jake replied. "Mrs. Colvert, the nurse who came in at noon is staying overnight in Mae's room. She couldn't make it home, and the night shift nurse couldn't get here anyway because of the weather. You'll want to check on Ina when you go upstairs, too. She has a migraine."

"Probably from worrying about me, knowing Ina," Joanna remarked. She turned and hurried up the steps.

"Joanna, is that you?" Ina's voice called out into the hallway.

"Yes, it's me. I'm sorry you were so worried." She walked into the bedroom. "Is your headache a bad one?"

"Oh, it's bad enough to keep me up here in my room for a while," she answered. Ina adjusted the ice bag she had on her head. "Sometimes cold helps, sometimes heat. This time, nothing seems to do the trick. I guess you and Dr. Barnes will be forced to spend the evening alone together," Ina commented with a sly grin. "The phones aren't working, so there won't be any interruptions from the hospital. And with the electricity off, all you need is the sun to go down for a romantic evening by candlelight."

"Ina, it's not that way with us," Joanna replied.

"Oh, pshaw! The trouble with you young people is you're too afraid of letting your feelings be known. By the time you reach my age, you'll learn not to waste time."

"I'm not even sure what my feelings are for him, Ina. I guess that's part of the reason I'm here." Joanna sighed. How much of a fool, she wondered, was she making out of herself by even being here, in Jake's house day after day?

"Dr. Barnes is a good man, Joanna. I like him very much, and he's much kinder, easier to work for than his grumpy father. But there's one thing that really concerns me. I probably shouldn't say anything about it, but..."

"Go ahead, Ina. Whatever it is, say it."

"Well, dear, he's not exactly open to the idea of allowing God into his life."

"He's not against it either," Joanna emphasized.

"He is very...undecided, I guess you could say. I've discussed it with him several times over the years."

"And he's shown interest?" Ina asked.

"He's interested. *Curious,* I guess would be a better word."

"When he told me you and Mae were coming here to stay until Mae's health improved, one of the first things he asked me was where I went to church. He said you'd want a place to attend. So I suggested that he go with you."

Joanna's mouth opened in surprise. "And he said...?"

"That he might."

"Wow," Joanna remarked and sat down on the edge of Ina's bed. "That's a new development."

Ina gave a slight shrug. "I think there's reason to be hopeful. In many ways."

Joanna studied her friend's smiling face and raised an eyebrow in mock suspicion. "That migraine couldn't be too bad, Ina, considering the amount of talking we've been doing."

"But it's bad enough to keep me out of your way for the evening," she responded with a wink. "Now, go have a nice chat with Dr. Barnes." She moved the ice bag from her head. "And don't tell him my comment about his father. It's not his fault that the man was an insufferable grouch."

"You know, he never talks about his parents. Either one of them," Joanna replied.

"I never knew his mother. I heard she died when Jake was a child. Andrew Vernon told me she was a very beautiful young woman."

"Maybe I'll ask him about her." Joanna stood up.

"You're going to need candles and matches, Joanna. They're both in the bottom drawer of the hall closet."

"Thanks, Ina. If you need anything, just say so. I'm sure I can hear you from downstairs." She walked toward the doorway. "Thanks for the advice."

"Any time, dear. Have a good evening."

Joanna gathered the items she needed from the hallway closet, then went into her room to change. The light-gray corduroys and pink sweater she slipped into felt much better than the clothing she'd taken off. She put on some soft gray socks and flats before brushing her hair and heading toward Mae's bedroom. But her aunt was sleeping again. It was getting dark outside by then, so she lit a candle and started downstairs.

"Jo, I'm in here."

She heard Jake call to her when she reached the bottom of the steps. She walked inside the study.

"Good, you found the candles. I couldn't locate anything but a couple of flashlights down here," Jake said when she entered the room.

"Ina told me where they were."

"Have a seat," Jake offered with a slight nod of his head in the direction of the couch.

She placed the burning candle on an end table and sank down into the plump cushions of the sofa, drawing her legs up under her. The fierce, howling wind pressed against the windowpanes causing an eerie creaking sound, and the entire house shuddered under the icy assault.

"There's tea on the table," Jake offered. Then he turned from the fireplace to join her.

Tea. Joanna looked at the cup for a moment. Tea was Natalie Eden's favorite drink. The doctor usually had a cup of it in her hand or sitting somewhere close by whenever Joanna had seen her at the clinic. Was Jake thinking of Natalie? Missing her on this snowy evening? She picked up the cup, warming her hands with the heat it offered. "How can we have tea?" she asked. "I thought the well wasn't working."

"You're forgetting the latest in modern technology," he said with a smile and sat down not far from her. "Bottled water. I heated it in a pan on the woodburner in the kitchen."

The golden firelight flickered throughout the darkened room, and Joanna watched Jake lean back against the sofa, a cup in one hand and the other arm stretched out along the back of the couch. He studied the dancing flames in silence.

"Do you think the house will be damaged from this wind?" Joanna asked.

"Not much. This place is over a hundred years old. I'm sure it's been through worse storms than this."

"The snow is beautiful. I've never seen so much of it at one time," Joanna commented, thinking of the depths of whiteness that blanketed the land for miles around them. "It's absolutely breathtaking."

Jake turned his head toward her, smiling in amusement.

"What's so funny?" she asked.

"It's been a long time since I've thought of a foot

of snow as breathtaking," he replied, his gray eyes shining with the reflection of the fireplace.

"But it is, Jake. And you grew up around it. Didn't you miss real winters like this when you were in South Carolina?"

"I didn't really miss anything, until I left South Carolina," he answered quietly.

"Do you miss working at the clinic?" she asked, curious about his statement. She couldn't bring herself to ask if he missed Dr. Eden. The answer would likely be something she didn't want to hear.

"Every day."

Jake had taken over his father's private practice with Dr. Andrew Vernon, his father's former associate, and Joanna had thought that was what he had honestly wanted to do. His candid reply surprised her.

"Why don't you work in a clinic here or start one yourself, if that's the kind of work you enjoy?" She watched his face brighten as he spoke briefly of possibilities he'd considered.

"There are so many areas around here that could use another good clinic like the one in South Carolina."

"But...why did you take over your father's practice here if your heart wasn't in it?"

"His dream was for us to work together and, eventually, for me to take over the practice. Of course, he never had the chance to retire. He died before I had agreed to work with him. A few months after his death, I decided I needed to come home for a while."

She gave a quiet sigh. How awful that must have felt. "I'm sorry it happened that way," she said softly as she watched his troubled gray eyes look past her toward the window, which displayed nothing but blackness.

She shifted positions, stretching her cramped legs out in front of her. "You've worked with Andrew for nearly two years. If you're not content with it by now, don't you think you should make a change?"

"Probably, but I keep trying to convince myself that if I stay with it long enough, eventually my heart will be in it." He shook his head and laughed at his own statement. "I know this sounds ridiculous, but I think I'm trying to make amends with my father for not being here when he wanted me." He looked into her eyes. "Do you know what I mean?"

"Yes." A thoughtful smile curved her mouth. "I understand, but I doubt that your father would want you to make anything up to him. He'd want you to be happy with your own life, Jake, not try to live his."

"I know what you're saying is true...but it doesn't feel that way. Dad and I never got along well together and the one thing he wanted most from me, I wouldn't do." Jake paused. "After he died, moving here—back to my hometown—and taking over for him seemed like the right thing to do. I think that's what I've been trying to do—the right thing."

Yes, Joanna recalled. Jake had decided to return to Indiana and had asked Natalie Eden to go with him. Joanna remembered Dr. Eden's words. Pushing thoughts of Natalie from her mind, she offered, "So you've tried to practice medicine your father's way, and you're not happy with it. At least check into the idea of a clinic. What do you have to lose?''

''The loss of income from a private practice would be astounding, Jo.''

If Jake held any hope of a future with Natalie Eden, income was a sacrifice he'd better think twice about making, Joanna considered. She'd seen the cars and jewelry that woman owned.

But Jake continued, ''If I make any major changes, I'd have to sell at least one of my father's farms to finance it.''

''They're not your father's any longer. He's gone, and whatever he left to you, belongs to you. Can you think of a better way to spend money than to invest in a clinic that would provide medical care for people who otherwise couldn't afford it?''

''It's not an easy decision to make,'' he replied with a gentle smile. ''But you can be a very convincing woman.'' He touched her chin, his fingers lingering against her skin for a warm, wonderful moment.

''People should try to do what's important to them,'' Joanna said, ''and working in a clinic sounds very important to you.''

''Social work means a lot to you, doesn't it,'' he stated more than asked.

''Yes. That's what I've always wanted to do. I've known since I was a little girl with a caseworker of my own that social work was the only job for me,'' she replied with confidence. Her commitment was very real to her, and it felt good to share it with someone.

A solemn look darkened Jake's features as he spoke. "You lived in foster care before you were adopted, didn't you?"

"Yes, there was some moving around, but I ended up in a pretty good home." Not particularly loving, but kind. Safe. Joanna averted her eyes to stare into the flames of the fireplace. Discussing the past was never easy.

Jake nodded silently. "Have you talked to them lately? Your adoptive parents, I mean?"

"No," Joanna answered. "After I found out about Aunt Mae, they were very upset that I'd gone against their wishes. They haven't answered any of my letters."

"Maybe," Jake began, "given enough time, they'll change their minds."

Joanna shook her head. "I don't think so. They aren't exactly lonely. They have a biological daughter who is married and has three children. She was an only child that they had late in life, and I think they adopted me more to be her playmate than because they wanted a second child." She took a sip of her tea. "Adoptions like that normally don't go well."

"How old were you when your natural parents died in the plane crash?"

"Almost four," came her quiet response. "So I was young just like you were when you lost your mother."

"Who told you that?" he asked quietly, drawing her attention from the amber glow of the crackling logs.

"Aunt Mae, I think. Does it matter?" She was

pleased he'd been so open with her all evening, but now she felt it slipping away.

"No," he answered, wondering how much he should explain. "It's just that...after she was gone, my father—" He stopped.

Studying the profile of his face against the firelight, Joanna refrained from asking any further questions. Tonight didn't feel like the right time.

Then he was looking at her again, the tenderness in his eyes reaching her very soul. "Some things aren't easy to talk about."

"That's very true," she responded.

"You know," he began as he touched her hand, linking his fingers through hers, "you really frightened me this afternoon. I thought I'd lost you out in that storm."

"I'm sorry," she answered, and it took all the strength she had not to lean toward him. Never in her life could she remember wanting to kiss, or to be kissed by anyone as much as she did in that moment.

Jake's gaze lowered to her softly parted lips for a moment as a similar thought must have crossed his mind; but he raised his gaze again quickly, concentrating on her luminous brown velvet eyes.

"I'm thankful to that God you serve for keeping you safe," he said as he released her hand and leaned back against the sofa in a more comfortable position. "Do you realize that in all the time I've known you, you've never criticized me for not going to church with you?"

Joanna ran her finger around the lip of the teacup she still held in one hand. At first, she had thought he was going to kiss her. Now, the conversation had taken a turn toward religion. He couldn't have confused her more if he had deliberately tried.

"I don't believe anyone should force their personal religious views on anyone else," she replied.

"I didn't know what to expect from you," he said, and she felt his mood changing slowly. "Dr. Eden told me that having you live here would be like having an evangelist take up residence in my home."

Anger instantly flushed her cheeks as she wondered what other things he and Dr. Eden had discussed concerning her. "Dr. Eden apparently has a way of exaggerating things."

"Now, there's the understatement of the year," he responded, his mouth curving upward in genuine amusement.

Joanna had no intention of discussing Dr. Natalie Eden tonight. If he wanted to think about her, he could do that all by himself. In the dark. She reached for the only candle in the room. "If you'll excuse me—"

"Don't go," he said, the smile gone. "I didn't mean to upset you."

"Christianity is a serious matter to me, Jake. I don't want to be teased about it," she explained.

"Stay with me," he urged. "I won't tease you."

She doubted his words, but she returned to her place on the sofa anyway, drawn to him in a way she wasn't sure she liked.

"I'm sorry. I know church is very important to you," he offered in a solemn voice. All humor was gone.

"Yes, church is important, but having a personal relationship with God, serving Him—those are the things that mean the most to me," Joanna spoke softly, almost reverently.

"And how do you serve Him?" Jake's eyes searched her face.

"I try to do what He wants me to do with my life," she responded.

"But how do you know what He wants from you? How does anyone know?" he asked.

"Pray, read the Bible," she began, but she had to look away from the deep gray of his distracting eyes before she could concentrate. "I try to be aware of what God-given talents I have and use them. Sometimes people aren't sure what He wants them to do, but the important thing is that they try." She met his eyes again only to see that the intensity of his gaze had not diminished, and her heart turned over in response.

"But you know, don't you?" he said.

"I know part of it. My education, even my work at Smithfield is all a part of the plan." She took a sip of her tea, then placed the cup on the table as Jake watched her movements.

"How long have you been...serious about religion?" he asked.

An involuntary smile crossed her lips as she realized he didn't know how to say it. "I've been a Christian since I was twelve. Do you believe in God, Jake?"

"Yes, I don't see how anyone in my profession could not believe." He paused. "Sometimes when we've done all we can by way of medicine, surgery, whatever…sometimes all we can do is stand back and hope that God intervenes.''

''And pray,'' she suggested.

Jake's mouth straightened into a thin line. ''I'm not a praying man, Jo, unless you count my feeble attempt at it today when I thought I'd never find you in that blizzard.''

Joanna's lips parted to respond, but no words came out. Jake had prayed for her safety, and he could not have said anything that meant more. Her eyes shimmered with unshed tears.

''Sometimes,'' he said, his darkening gaze holding hers easily, ''when I look at you…'' Then he leaned forward, his mouth meeting hers in a kiss, gentle and far sweeter, than either of them remembered.

Instinctively, Joanna reached for him. Her arms slid tentatively around his neck as she felt his hands move against the back of her soft sweater. The lingering caress of Jake's mouth against hers ignited a warmth that spread through Joanna slowly but steadily, and her willing response only deepened their longing for one another.

''Jo…'' he spoke her name again quietly as he brought the sweet intimacy to a reluctant end. But he didn't pull away from her. Not this time. Instead they leaned together, forehead to forehead, as they both caught their breath. ''Why do I keep letting this happen?'' he asked himself in no more than a husky whisper.

The truth Joanna had tried to ignore, came clearly to the surface. ''Because this is what we want, Jake.''

He gave a quiet groan and pulled away from her slightly, placing a hand on either side of her face. He looked straight into her dark eyes. "Don't say that. It's impossible."

"Why? Don't you feel it, too? There's something between us that won't go away. No matter how much we want it to."

"You don't understand," he said. She didn't know how it felt to see a father fall apart right in front of your eyes, and all because of a lost love, he longed to say as he looked into her youthful face. Her eyes, her smile, even those soft hands that he'd pulled away from—everything spoke of her young years, her unsettled choices. What she wanted at twenty-two, she might not want at thirty-two. And it would nearly kill him, he knew, to let her go then. It was all he could do to walk away now. Without really having her. "Jo, you can't understand how I feel about you," he began, searching for the right words. "I've known you since you were eighteen—"

"I'm not a teenager anymore, Jake. I barely had the chance to be a kid, when I was a kid considering the way I grew up. I'm not immature or silly or frivolous...whatever it is you think a twenty-two-year-old should be."

"Of course, you're not." She was none of those things. "You're the hardest working, most mature twenty-two-year-old I've ever known." But enough so to be sure of what she wanted in life? He doubted it.

"Then don't make it sound so impossible. I mean,

I know I'm not Dr. Natalie Eden. I'm not as attractive, as sophisticated, as well-educated—''

"She has nothing to do with us," Jake remarked.

"Doesn't she?" Joanna asked sharply. "She's better for you than I am on every level. She has about a decade more experience at everything than I have—''

"Don't be ridiculous," Jake cut off her words.

"Then what is it? First you want me, then you don't." Joanna raised her hands in a helpless gesture.

"I always want you," he admitted as though it would be some consolation, all the while knowing the want wasn't half the pain that the love he was beginning to feel for her was proving to be. "I've never known you to do anything wrong in your life, Joanna." Running a hand through his disheveled hair, he stood up and walked toward the fireplace. "And you're not going to start now, not with me."

"Is that what you think? That you're responsible for my behavior? That I have no Christian standards, Jake?" she said tersely. "That I'd do whatever you wanted? Well, you're mistaken."

Jake looked over his shoulder at her with a frown. "I didn't say that—'' No, but he knew in his heart he'd thought it, worried about it—not fully trusting himself with that responsibility.

"You think it. And, why? Because I enjoy kissing you so much?" Inwardly, she cringed at the sound of her words. How she wished she hadn't said such a childish thing, especially when she'd been trying to prove exactly how immature she *wasn't*. She stood up, reaching for the candle. Thankfully, the shadows of the room hid the blush that burned her cheeks.

Raising a hand to shield the flame from blowing out, she took a step toward the doorway. "I'm not some little girl you have to protect," Joanna assured him, "I know what I'm doing, and I'm quite capable of taking care of myself." She blinked hard, fighting the temptation to cry. She couldn't remember ever feeling more foolish in all her life.

Jake stared at her with a melancholy expression. "I shouldn't have let this happen between us again," he said quietly. "Being here, alone together...I knew it wasn't wise."

She turned and looked into the reflection of firelight dancing in his eyes. "Don't apologize. Just don't think you know more about me than I do. I'm young, but I'm not a child, Jake."

"I'm very aware of that," he admitted as some unspoken pain shadowed his troubled expression. It seemed every time he came near her, he ended up regretting it. But none, more than tonight. "But you are so young...too young to be with someone my age."

"I don't think age has anything to do with this. It's just a convenient excuse." She gave a hopeless sigh. "If two people fall in love, what difference does it make what ages they are?"

He hesitated, measuring her words. Was she saying she loved him? At her tender age, how could she know? "Have you ever been in love?" The unexpected question came from his heart not his head, and he wished he hadn't asked it.

"No," she answered truthfully. Until you, she thought miserably. "But we've been friends for so long, Jake. I know the man you are, and I trust you. Maybe that's what makes everything feel so different with you."

Jake's eyes held hers. Different, how? He wanted to know. Could it be what she felt for him would last forever? Could he trust her judgment? His father had taken that chance. And the price he'd paid had been high. Too high. "Joanna, you deserve a future with a man who thinks like you do, believes in the things you believe in. With me...you wouldn't have that. I don't want you to get hurt."

Her eyes were pools of tears, and the knowledge that he'd caused them brought a searing stab of guilt in his chest.

"And that's what you think you'll do, Jake? Hurt me?"

He flinched at the sound of her words. No, he'd never hurt her. Not intentionally. But her heart wasn't the only one at stake. It was himself he was protecting as much as her. "I don't want to find out."

Joanna nodded after listening to his reply. "You're not my guardian. You don't have to look after me, you know."

"No," he agreed. Maybe a dose of honesty was his only alternative. "It's not only you I'm protecting. It's me, too. I don't want to get married, settle down, have a family. Those things aren't in my plans, Joanna." And she made him want them.

She stared at him in astonishment, momentarily speechless in response. Just when she thought she understood his motives, he surprised her completely with the truth. "Jake...I didn't come here with the thought of forever in my mind. I came because Aunt Mae wanted me to come.'' She swallowed at the lump in her throat as her heart pounded furiously with more truth. ''And I guess I came here for myself, too. I needed to know what there was—what there could be—between us. I've wondered since that night.''

''I've thought a lot about it,'' he replied. Too much, he knew. ''But we're friends. I value that more than I do a passing romance.''

Joanna cleared her throat nervously. ''And passing is all it would be?''

Jake looked directly into her luminous eyes. ''That's all either of us has ever known.''

''But our friendship—'' she began.

''Is something I don't want to lose, Jo. And we will,'' he said and reached out, caressing her cheek, ''if we let this happen.''

His eyes, dark with anguish, mesmerized her. She raised a hand, her fingers covering his where they touched her face.

''I'm sorry, Jo.''

She nodded and lowered her hand back to her side, watching him turn from her to return to his place near the crackling logs. There he stood, staring into the flames.

She took a deep breath of reality. This was the end of whatever she'd hoped for. It felt final. Painful, but final and maybe that was good. Jake couldn't make his heart feel something it wouldn't feel. She wouldn't want him to try. More hot tears burned her eyes. She blinked hard, wishing them away.

''Good night, Jake,'' was all she could say. Then

Joanna left him standing in the glow of the fire-light…alone. Which was how it should be, she reminded herself as she climbed the stairs. That's how he wanted it. Maybe now he would feel as alone as she did at this very moment.

Chapter Five

Several days passed, and Joanna's work at Smithfield got off to a very good start. The chill between Joanna and Jake, however, had not subsided. She wasn't sure it ever would. If Mae didn't improve enough to return home soon, Joanna wasn't certain what she was going to do. She should probably look for a cheap apartment nearby to wait out the rest of her aunt's recovery time. Or maybe she should go back to Mae's home. At least it was paid for, so rent wouldn't be a problem, and she could leave her aunt in Jake's care. She was upstairs with Mae, pondering her situation for about the hundredth time when Ina's voice caught her attention.

"Joanna, dear, would you mind dropping something off at the office on your way to work?" Ina called up the staircase.

Joanna stuck her head out of the doorway. "Jake's office?" she asked.

"Yes, these papers came in the mail a few minutes ago. He mentioned them this morning at the breakfast table, so I think he might need them today."

Joanna had no idea what Jake may have mentioned at breakfast. She had not shared a meal with him since that snowy evening they'd shared by the firelight. All encounters they had experienced since that night had been cordial, brief and mostly accidental. Nothing more.

"I don't know, Ina. He might not appreciate my showing up at his office. Maybe you should take it to him."

Ina protested, "But it won't take you more than ten minutes out of your way, and I have too many things to do today to go downtown."

"All right," Joanna told her, but it really wasn't all right. She'd avoided Jake as best she could lately, and the thought of deliberately walking into his office—his domain—was unsettling.

"It will only take you a few minutes," Ina encouraged, reading the concern on Joanna's face. "If he's too busy to be bothered with it, just leave the papers with the receptionist."

"Excellent idea," she answered as she hurried down the steps. "I'll drop them off at the front desk." Joanna paused in front of the large oval mirror hanging on the living room wall and surveyed her reflection quickly. Her hair hung to her shoulders in its usual soft blond curls and her blush and lipstick were acceptable. But she knew she owned prettier sweaters than the powder-blue one she was wearing. And these old jeans, she thought as she glanced down...

"You seem quite concerned about your appearance for someone who is merely dropping something off at the front desk," Ina commented, catching Joanna's eyes in the mirror.

Joanna gave a sheepish smile. "You should always look your best, Ina," she explained with an embarrassed shrug. "No matter what you are doing."

"Or whom you'll be seeing?" Ina added and handed her the large manila envelope. "Dear, I don't know what went on between you and Dr. Barnes the other night, but— "

"It was nothing important," Joanna replied.

"Is that why breakfast is being eaten in shifts nowadays?"

"We had a misunderstanding, that's all," Joanna answered, all the while knowing it was only a half truth at best.

"A misunderstanding about what?"

"About exactly what you might expect. I'm falling in love with him, Ina, and the feelings aren't exactly reciprocal." Even saying the words hurt. "All he wants is my friendship. Dr. Natalie Eden is the right woman for Jake. At least all signs point in that direction." She pulled her gloves on quickly. "He doesn't want to admit it, but I think he's in love with her."

"Oh, for heaven's sake, Joanna," Ina gave an immediate reaction. "He's no more in love with a Dr. Natalie Eden than...than I am! You don't really believe that, do you? Do you even know this woman?"

"She was Aunt Mae's doctor in the clinic in Charleston. I know her well enough to know she has her eye on Jake. Again. He wanted her to move back here with him when he took over his father's practice a couple of years ago, but she refused. Apparently, now, she's having second thoughts.'' Joanna took a deep breath. "Okay, I've explained what the problem is, now you'll understand why things aren't so cozy between us. May I go now?'' Joanna's tone sounded dejected.

"Give him time, dear,'' Ina said without hesitation. "I don't recall ever hearing him mention anything to me about Natalie Eden. And, even if he did have a relationship with her, that's in the past. He's surely gotten over it by now."

"Do people always get over it?'' Joanna asked and searched Ina's face for the impossible answer.

"Jake will,'' came a certain response, "but I just can't believe you're right about this, Joanna."

"I *am* right, Ina. The only thing wrong in all of this is how deeply I care about him. He doesn't share my Christian beliefs, my values. We're not right for each other, but I didn't intend to feel this way. It just happened. He was there and I was there and now... Love is so...so..."

"Difficult to explain sometimes,'' Ina said, finishing the thought. "I know, dear. Sometimes it comes and goes, but sometimes it stays forever."

Joanna didn't know whether to laugh or cry. Which was it for Jake and Natalie Eden? Which was it for her own broken heart?

"Did you tell Jake you're in love with him?'' Ina asked.

"No," she replied. She had not told him; she'd spared herself from that humiliation.

"Well, you should. I've seen how he is around you. You can't tell me he's not attracted to you. Maybe if he knew—"

"It wouldn't make any difference." Joanna opened the door to leave. "The only reason I'm a part of his life now is because of Aunt Mae's insistence that I come along with her. My presence in this house has nothing to do with me personally."

"I don't agree with that. Talk to him, Joanna. Do something about this misunderstanding."

"I'm trying to do something about it. I'm trying to work all the hours available so I can afford to get out of here. I need to find a place of my own or go back home until Aunt Mae is well enough to leave."

"Don't rush things, Joanna. Give Mae a little more time. Stay here with her. She counts on you being around. And in the meantime, tell Dr. Barnes that you're in love with him," Ina continued in her usual persistent manner. "He deserves to know the truth about your feelings."

"I've got to go or I'll be late, Ina. I'll see you tonight," Joanna told her before stepping out into the crisp morning air. Tell Jake she loved him? Now? After all that had happened?

"And be sure to tell Andrew I said hello," Ina called out the door after her.

Now, there was a message she could deliver, and she assured Ina she would. In fact, with any luck, maybe hello was more than she'd have to say to Jake.

The drive to the office shared by Dr. Barnes and Dr. Vernon took about half an hour, and soon Joanna was on the elevator heading for the fourth floor. She had been to the office only once shortly after she'd moved here. Ina had stopped in briefly on one of their outings and given her a quick tour. It took Joanna several minutes to find the correct suite this time, but finally she opened the door. Then she walked through the crowded reception area to the front desk.

This could turn out to be easy after all, she was thinking when the slender young woman behind the desk asked, "Do you have an appointment?"

"No, I want to leave this for Dr. Barnes. He's expecting it," Joanna said as she looked down at the envelope in her hand rather than into the gorgeous blue eyes of this attractive woman who worked with Jake. Every day. Joanna couldn't recall meeting this receptionist when she'd toured the office. And this female wasn't likely to be forgotten.

"Joanna?"

She glanced up to see Andrew Vernon, Jake's associate, walking toward her. "Hello, Dr. Vernon. I'm surprised you recognized me."

"Of course, I recognize you. How could I not remember a beautiful young woman like yourself?" the older gentleman said as he opened the side door to the staff area. "And, please, call me Andrew." He motioned her inside the door. "How are Mae and Ina?"

"They're both doing well," Joanna replied. "Ina asked me to say hello for her."

"Good, good. Tell her I asked about her. Come on in. I'll get Jake for you."

"No, please, don't bother him," Joanna quickly protested. "I only need to drop off these papers—"

"Nonsense. You're not a bother. Come in here," he insisted.

"No, really, I—" She wished she were back on the elevator. Going down.

"Jake," he said. Joanna cringed at the sound of Andrew's voice calling his partner, but she stepped inside the doorway away from the curious eyes of a waiting room filled with people. "Come here for a minute, Jake. There's someone here to see you."

There was nothing she could do to avoid the awkwardness of this situation but smile and pretend she was not dying on the inside. "Hi," she offered weakly as Jake walked around the corner in response to Andrew's words.

He was wearing his glasses and a typical white jacket over his clothes and carrying a medical chart in one hand. "Hello," he responded when his questioning eyes met hers.

Andrew continued, "Now, this is a pleasant surprise, Jake. I'm sure this young pretty lady can put you in a better mood. I have a patient waiting, so I'll leave you two alone."

They were hardly alone. The lovely receptionist was within hearing range of every word spoken, and there must have been a dozen people in the waiting room on the other side of the partition.

"I didn't mean to disturb you, Jake. Ina asked me to bring this to you. She said you've been waiting for it."

Jake slid the chart under one arm, holding it there

while he opened the large manila envelope Joanna had handed him. He glanced at the papers and then slid them back into the envelope, smiling as he did so.

A man and young boy came from one of the nearby examining rooms and approached the receptionist as Joanna was about to speak.

"Thank you, Dr. Barnes," the man said as he extended a hand toward Jake.

"You're welcome, George. We'll see you and Timmy early next week," was Jake's response, accompanied by a smile.

"Yep, thanks, Doc," the youngster added.

Jake squeezed the child's shoulder gently. "Sure thing, Tim. See you next time."

The man was writing a check and scheduling another appointment, and Joanna did not want to say anything more in front of complete strangers. "I'll see you later," she spoke to Jake as she started for the door.

"No, wait," he said, and he motioned toward the empty examining room that the man and his son had vacated. "C'mere."

She followed him into the room and watched him close the door. Jake placed the chart and envelope on the table in the small, antiseptic-smelling room.

"I don't suppose you know what's in that envelope," he said.

"No, I don't read your mail," she answered, watching his laughing eyes. "But Ina said you'd been waiting for it."

"That's true, I suppose," he responded. "I wait

anxiously every year for my accountant to send my income tax forms to me.''

''Income tax? But that's not due—''

''For quite a while,'' he concluded her thought with a broad smile. ''Not exactly an urgent piece of mail.''

''But the way Ina explained it, I thought it was.''

''I'm sure you did,'' he said as he sat down and removed his glasses, turning them over in his hands. ''Ina probably wants us to talk. She's convinced that you and I...'' He didn't need to finish the sentence. He looked up at her and the sudden seriousness in his eyes was sufficient.

''I know,'' Joanna replied softly, nervously. She averted her gaze to the scale a few feet away.

''She means well,'' Jake added.

''I suppose.'' How Joanna wished this discussion would end. Her heart thumped so loudly within her she could barely think.

''Things have been a little tense since the other night,'' he said as he stood up, retrieving the chart and envelope from the table.

''That's mostly my fault.'' Joanna knew she had been difficult to get along with since she realized she was in love with a man who would never love her.

''It's been my fault, too, but we're going to be living together for a while, Jo. However long Mae needs us.'' He tapped the envelope he held in his hand. ''Maybe even past income tax time.''

She looked up, relaxing a little when she saw his warm smile. ''I'd like to move out, Jake, but so far I'm not working enough hours at Smithfield to make that possible. But maybe I should just go back to Charleston."

"No. I don't want you to leave," he stated firmly. "Not yet."

Joanna shook her head. "It would be easier for us."

"We've been friends a long time, Jo. We can work through this. Mae needs you here."

She nodded her head reluctantly. Even if she'd wanted to differ with him, her arguments and options were few.

"I'm working late tonight. But tomorrow evening, I should be home by six o'clock. Will you have dinner with me then?" he asked, surprising her with the question. Her startled look made him laugh quietly. "It's not that unusual, is it? We have eaten together before, you know."

"All right," she responded. Heartbreak, round three. Or was it four? She'd lost count. But the meals they'd shared before that snowy evening had been pleasant enough. She hoped they could be again despite the distance that night had created between them.

They walked to the door together, and he pulled it open for her to step out into the hallway. "I'll see you later."

The woman at the front desk eyed her curiously, and Joanna forced a smile in return. "I apologize for not recognizing you, Miss Meccord," the receptionist said in a hollow tone of voice that Joanna didn't appreciate. "Dr. Vernon explained to me that you've been here before, but I really can't recall ever meeting you."

"That's quite all right," Joanna replied, "I don't remember you, either." She turned to exit through the side door and saw Jake standing in the hallway, smiling in amusement at her words.

Chapter Six

Joanna hurried up the sidewalk toward the back door of Smithfield. Anxious to get inside, out of the wind, she pulled open the large double doors and was nearly blown into the building by a strong gust.

"Jo-Jo? Ready to go?" called an excited young voice from inside the door.

Running her fingers through her tangled curls, she replied, "Hi, guys. I'll be ready in a minute." Shaking her head briskly in an effort to let her hair fall back into its natural place, she nearly lost her balance when she was grabbed around the knees in a fierce hug by a little boy.

"Hey, now," she said with a laugh. "Give a girl a break, will ya?" She freed herself from his grasp and knelt to the floor, opening her arms. "Instead of tackling me, how about a real hug?"

The six-year-old blond boy flew into her arms immediately, asking as he snuggled close, "Are you ready to go now?"

"You're terribly excited about going out to buy a pair of shoes, aren't you?" she commented, and not waiting for the obvious reply, she continued, "I'll be ready as soon as I get the keys to the van. Have you been waiting long?"

"Yes!" the child replied. "For a long, long time."

"For about five minutes, Freddie," responded another adult.

"Hello, Barbara." Joanna glanced at the co-worker who had entered the living area of the child care facility. "Five minutes, huh? That doesn't sound like a long, long time to me, kiddo."

Freddie giggled and ran to the couch to pick up his jacket.

"Freddie, where's Aaron? He's supposed to go with us," Joanna asked when she did not see the other child anywhere in the room.

Aaron was the new admission Joanna had met only briefly. He was an unusually quiet child whom Joanna had developed an instant liking for the moment they had been introduced.

Barbara answered instead of Freddie. "Aaron's getting his coat. He'll be ready in a minute. I've got to get back to the other children in the gym. Bob's all by himself down there with them." Barbara pulled her dark hair up into a ponytail as she spoke. "By the way, Bob's been asking questions about you." She grinned.

"What kind of questions?" Joanna asked while heading toward the office. She pulled a set of keys from the pocket of her jeans and unlocked the office door.

"Oh, little things like—where is she from, what's her favorite restaurant, is she dating anyone?" Barbara slipped the plastic clip around her hair. "Things like that."

"South Carolina, don't have one and no," Joanna provided the answers with a friendly smile. "And I'm not looking for anyone to date. Maybe you could mention that to him, too, Barb. In a nice, polite, subtle kind of way?"

Barbara laughed. "What? You don't approve of my usual blunt style?"

"Bob's a nice guy. I don't want to hurt his feelings."

"And what can I tell him about this relationship of yours with the doctor you're living with?" Barbara asked with a dramatic lifting of her eyebrows.

"Just say I'm staying at his house for a while, Barb. So are Ina, Aunt Mae and an assortment of round-the-clock nurses. It's not exactly a cozy little arrangement. We're not 'living together' in the way that you mean."

"If you say so," Barb responded with a mischievous grin.

"Oh, by the way," Joanna explained, "I'm taking both boys to buy tennis shoes today, but we won't be gone over an hour."

"Okay, see you later," Barbara called over her shoulder as she headed out of the living area. "And about Bob—I'll try to break it to him gently."

Glancing over the chart of available vehicles, she saw that all the vans were signed out for the afternoon. "I guess we'll have to take my car," she called

out to Freddie, then added, "if I have enough gaso-
line." She tried to remember what the gas gauge read
when she had looked at it earlier that day. Then, out
of the corner of her eye, she saw Aaron walk out of
the bedroom he shared with Freddie. She smiled but
bit her lip to keep a laugh from escaping as Aaron
appeared dressed not only in a jacket, but also in a
winter cap, gloves and a scarf wrapped securely
around his neck as though he were ready to brave the
harshest blizzard.

"Hi there, little guy," she said as he peered out at
her from the small space he'd left between the bottom
of his heavy winter stocking cap and the top of his
neck scarf.

"My name isn't Guy. It's Aaron," he answered in
a quiet, matter-of-fact manner as though she simply
had been mistaken.

"I know your name is Aaron, but I just meant—"
She stopped in midsentence, looking down into his
quizzical expression and decided it was not worth explaining. "Let's start over. Hi, Aaron," she tried
again.

"Hello, Jo-Jo," he responded politely.

"Hey, Aaron." Freddie was off the couch at first
sight of his roommate, and Joanna knew what was
coming next. "What are you wearing all that stuff
for? You look gross!"

Joanna intervened immediately. "Well, I don't
think *gross* is a good description, but you really don't
need all those clothes on today, Aaron." She reached
for the scarf around his neck, unwinding it gently.

"But I don't want to get cold," Aaron insisted.

"You won't. I promise," she said and as she raised her hand to pull the cap from his head, he jerked his face away from her raising his own arm in a protective gesture. Joanna froze, recognizing the meaning of Aaron's reaction.

Instantly he dropped his arm to his side and stood as straight and tall as his small frame would allow, apparently embarrassed by his instinctive actions.

"What's the matter with you?" Freddie fired the question at Aaron after noticing his roommate's unusual behavior. Placing his pudgy little hands on his hips, he imitated one of the night supervisor's frequent poses. "Jo-Jo won't hit you. She won't hit nobody."

"Freddie, back on the couch, please," Joanna ordered. She smiled at Aaron when she knelt on the carpet in front of him, coming eye to eye with the nervous youngster. "Why don't you take off your hat, and your gloves, too, Aaron. It's windy outside but not very cold, so you won't need them today. The weather has warmed up a lot."

After Aaron pulled his hat from his head, she warned him of her next move. "Here, let's straighten up your hair a bit." And this time when she raised her hand, he didn't budge. Fussing with his red curls, she studied the freckled face and said in a soothing voice, "You know, Aaron, you're safe here." Sorrow shot through her at the sound of her own words and the wary look in his clear green eyes. She knew, as he did, the promise was only for here and now; there were no guarantees for a lifetime. "No one here at Smithfield will ever hurt you," she added, hating the inadequacy of the statement. A six-year-old boy deserved better than that.

"I might," came a response from the direction of the sofa. "If he don't keep his junk on his side of the room, I'm gonna clobber him."

"Freddie." Joanna stood up as she spoke. "Do you want to go shopping with me—ever again?"

"Yes, ma'am," Freddie replied. "I'll shut up."

"Thank you," Joanna responded, and as she looked from Freddie's mischievous expression to Aaron's haunting green eyes, she knew this would be one of her longest days yet at Smithfield, even if it was only a six-hour shift.

It was late afternoon when Jake arrived home from the hospital that day. He found Ina sitting alone at the dining room table.

She was quick to explain, "I didn't expect you home so soon. Joanna is upstairs in her room so I decided to eat alone."

"That's fine, Ina," he replied, loosening his tie as he spoke. "Joanna has already had dinner?"

"No," Ina answered. "She said she wasn't hungry, but I'm worried about her."

Jake removed his jacket and pulled the tie free from his shirt. "Isn't she feeling well?"

"I don't know. She came home from work this afternoon, spent about an hour with Mae and then disappeared into her bedroom. I haven't seen her since then. I tried to talk her into eating a sandwich, but she said no. I think something happened at Smithfield today that's upset her."

"I wouldn't be surprised," he replied sharply. "That's exactly why I didn't want her working there. She doesn't need to relive the pain of her own childhood through the eyes of those kids." Jake collected his coat, tie and briefcase before walking from the dining room into his study. He was placing his jacket on the back of a large swivel desk chair when he noticed Ina had followed him and was standing inside the doorway.

"I know you don't approve of Joanna working at Smithfield but something has upset her, and she won't discuss it with me. I really wish you would go upstairs and talk to her."

Jake placed his briefcase on the floor next to his desk. "Why don't you finish your dinner before it gets cold? I'll see how she is."

Ina returned to her half-eaten meal, and Jake climbed the stairs slowly, knowing there was probably nothing he could say that would cause Joanna to confide in him any more readily than in Ina. He rapped his knuckles lightly against the door.

"Joanna, it's me. Are you okay?"

"Yes, I'm resting."

"According to Ina, you've been resting all afternoon. Are you sure you're feeling well?"

"Yes, I'm fine," she called from the other side of the door. "I'm just tired."

He paused for a few minutes, uncertain whether to pursue this matter or leave her in the privacy to which she was entitled.

"You'd make Ina a very happy woman if you'd agree to have some dinner," he said. "From looking at the food she had on her plate, I'd say she's having some kind of stew. But I warn you, I didn't ask... I'm only guessing.''

Her light laughter filtered through the barrier between them before she opened the door a few inches. Although sorrow had her heart in its grip that day, she smiled up at him, focusing on his steel-gray eyes. It was the concern she saw in the depths of those eyes that erased any remaining tension from the words they had exchanged on that cold, snowy evening not long ago.

''Why are you making fun of Ina's beef stew? You know she's a good cook,'' she countered, glad for the smile he'd brought to her lips.

''Sure, the food tastes good, but it's not always recognizable at first glance.'' Nodding toward the inside of her room, he asked, ''Could I come in for a minute?''

She hesitated only a moment, then opened the door wider. ''Come in, but don't step on the pictures.''

Jake entered the room, only to find that he had to watch his step to avoid the photographs scattered haphazardly over the plush apricot carpeting. ''What is all of this?''

Joanna sat down cross-legged on the floor in one of the few clutter-free places left. Sliding a bunch of photos to the side, she cleared a space for him. ''They're pictures.''

''That's obvious,'' he commented, taking a place beside her on the floor. ''What caused you to lock yourself in here all afternoon with a bunch of photographs?''

She had invited him, she reminded herself. Now, she would have to explain. "I don't like to admit this to you," she began in a faltering voice, "because I know how you feel about my job, but I met a little boy at work. You haven't seen him yet. He just arrived yesterday, but..."

Joanna could feel Jake's eyes resting intently on her as she spoke, and she fumbled with the pictures in her hand. "He's such a sad, little fellow, only six years old with bright red hair and the clearest green eyes I've ever seen. And, Jake..." She paused, fearing her voice would crack with emotion or that the tears would return. "When I read his chart...when I found out what he's been through... You can't imagine the things that have happened to him in those six years."

Jake offered no reply.

"I've been sitting here thinking." She paused until her voice steadied. "I'm thankful that nothing like that ever happened to me when I was growing up, but at the same time wondering why things like that happen to any child?"

Exactly what Jake had predicted would happen to her, had happened, and now she waited for him to tell her she had been warned of the heartache. But those words did not come.

"I'm sorry you're going through this," Jake said quietly. "What's his name?"

"Aaron," she spoke the little boy's name gently and wondered if anyone else ever had.

"Aaron," Jake repeated. "I'm sorry for Aaron, too."

The kindness in his voice increased the steady beat of her heart. Just when she thought she could stop loving this man, he proved her wrong.

Leaning back against the dresser behind him, Jake silently gathered up a few of the photographs from the floor. He shuffled through three, four, then five photos and found that a dark-eyed little girl stared out at him from each picture, different ages in various photos and each snapshot offered a different set of adults, but the child with the lonely eyes was unmistakably the same.

"These pictures…" He glanced up at Joanna to see the fading sunlight sifting through her soft blond hair, and sadness settled over him as those same dark eyes from the photographs looked cautiously at him now from the face of a young woman. "They're pictures of you," he concluded his thought audibly.

Joanna merely nodded her head and blinked hard at the sting in her eyes. She was not sure she wanted to share her past with him, although she knew he had not invaded her memories. She had invited him.

"Why?" he asked quietly with a grim expression stealing over his face, snatching away any trace of a smile. He glanced briefly again at one of the snapshots, realizing now these were fragments of her childhood he held in his hands. "Why are you doing this to yourself, Jo? It will only bring back bad memories."

Dropping her gaze from him, she focused on the pictures in his hands. "Not all of the memories are bad ones," she answered. Pointing to the top photo in Jake's grasp, she explained in a voice that sounded artificially calm, "Those were my adoptive parents, the Meccords." She picked up another picture from the floor. "And these are the Falks. I was with them in foster care when I was four...and that was my caseworker, Pam."

Jake watched her gather up several of the photographs and stack them into a neat, orderly pile with unsteady hands. He hesitated before speaking, not wanting to pry into a past she might not be ready to share. "Did they... Were these people good to you?"

"Yes, mostly they were," she answered, and although she felt the weight of his gaze upon her, she did not look up at him.

"No one ever hurt you?"

"No," she assured him. "Not in the way that you mean." Joanna turned to the side and pulled back the sheer, flower-print curtain to look out at the setting sun. "The worst part of it was feeling different from other children. Kind of like I never really belonged."

Jake sat silently, listening to her quiet words.

"Everything worked out for me. I don't know how it will be for Aaron," Joanna said in a voice edged with sorrow. "I just don't know," she added before a flood of warm tears filled her eyes.

"C'mere," he whispered, drawing her close in an instinctive gesture. He would have done anything to help her, and she knew it. Sitting huddled there against him, she wept until there were no more tears.

Some time later, she quieted in the comfort of his arms.

"Are you okay?" he asked. His breath stirred her hair.

Joanna nodded as she straightened and dried her eyes with a crumpled tissue. "I'm sorry. I didn't mean to cry all over you." She glanced up at him with tear-rimmed eyes. "There's lipstick on your shirt," she said as she reached to touch the spot. "At least..." She thought it was hers. She raised her uncertain gaze to meet his eyes.

"It doesn't matter," he replied regarding the stain. Then he saw with clarity the unspoken question in her dark eyes. "And it wouldn't be anyone else's." His unsmiling mouth captured her attention.

Her mind registered the meaning of his words, and she was relieved. But not hopeful. Her crazy mixture of hope and uncertainty had been doused that night beside the fireplace. They weren't meant for each other, and he'd made that clear. But still, she was grateful she didn't have to see him love someone else. She would be gone, safely back home in South Carolina before that happened, if she could manage it.

Jake covered her hand with his own. "You're allowed to cry on my shoulder whenever you need to," he replied with a tender smile. He gave her fingers an affectionate squeeze. "But I hate to see you sad, Joanna. I wish I could keep you from it. Always."

"You have high aspirations," she remarked with a smile. "Unreachable ones, I'd say."

"No harm in dreaming," he replied.

They sat silently for a time with Joanna leaning her head against his shoulder before either felt like speaking again.

"I know what you're thinking," she finally said. "'Such a short time on this job and already she's heartbroken.' You told me it would be like that, but I wouldn't listen.''

Jake couldn't deny it. Avoiding heartache had been his specialty. Until Joanna. "Why don't you find something less difficult to do?"

"Because I want to do this, Jake. It's the right job for me even if it makes me cry once in a while. Doesn't your work ever make you sad?"

"Of course it does," he answered. "That's why I hate so much for you to go through this. I know how awful it can be."

"But you wouldn't let yourself come home and cry," Joanna remarked. When Jake did not answer, she looked up at him again.

"I went through something like this the first time I watched a patient die."

Joanna stared, speechless. Somehow, she had never envisioned him as anything other than strong. Determined. Unyielding to any emotion he chose not to give in to. Maybe she'd been wrong.

"I was working in the emergency room one day. It was a car accident," he explained. "A young woman and her two little boys. The mother had brought the younger boy in earlier that week with an ear infection, so I knew them...recognized them." Jake picked up one of the stray photographs left lying on the floor and slowly turned it over and over in his hand. "Toby. That was his name. His mother and brother weren't seriously injured, but Toby...he didn't live through the afternoon."

Joanna reached to touch his arm gently.

"I wondered why God, if there even was a God,

would allow things like that to happen, why I had ever wanted to study medicine. Lord knows there must have been a million thoughts running through my mind that day,'' Jake said, his voice low and re-mote. "None of them good.''

Joanna said nothing as Jake placed the photograph on the floor and covered her hand with his own. "At the end of my shift, I went home and drank until that little face wasn't so clear in my mind any more. Then…sometimes crying is the only thing left to do.''

She nodded in wordless agreement, and Jake squeezed her fingers.

"That's all the sadness I can take for today, Jo.'' He stood up and tugged on her hand, pulling her to her feet. "Let's take a chance on some of Ina's beef stew.''

"I'd like that,'' she agreed. Joanna picked up the pictures quickly, placing them on top of her dresser. Then she walked down the staircase with Jake toward the dining room.

The tender moments shared in her room that day made Joanna hope that, no matter what else happened, she wouldn't lose Jake's friendship. She'd grown ac-customed to it again so quickly, it would be unimag-inable to let go.

It was early Sunday morning before she saw Jake again for anything more than a quick hello or good-bye. She was still adjusting the waistband of her straight jade-green skirt when she walked into the kitchen. "Oh, good morning, Jake. I didn't realize you were down here.''

He looked up from the newspaper he'd been reading. "You're going to church?" he asked, his brows slanting into a frown.

"Yes. It's Sunday," she replied, wondering why he was asking the needless question.

"But I thought after what happened with Aaron... I mean, it was only three days ago that you were asking how God could allow such sorrow in a little boy's life. I didn't think you'd be going back to church so soon."

Joanna slid her car keys into the pocket of her matching suit jacket. "I can't give up my faith in the Lord because of things I don't understand. I trust Him, even if I'm still questioning things."

He studied her curiously for a moment.

Picking up her purse and her Bible, Joanna turned to go. "See you later."

"Jo," he began, then glanced down at the casual shirt and slacks he was wearing. "If you wait for a few minutes while I change, I'd like to go with you."

She was too surprised to do more than nod before he disappeared through the doorway. She could hardly believe what Jake had said.

"I'm ready, Joanna," Ina called. She entered the kitchen from the back porch. "The car is running."

"Jake's going with us this morning," Joanna told her, knowing that the shock probably still registered in her eyes.

Ina's mouth dropped open momentarily. "Well... that's wonderful! Unusual, but wonderful." Then Ina offered, "I'll go ahead in my own car. I'll see you two later at church."

"There's no need to go in separate cars. You can ride with us."

"No, I don't want to be late, and I will be if I wait on both of you."

Joanna knew that this thoughtful friend of hers had little concern about arriving anywhere on time. More than a few times, she and Ina had hurried into various services already underway.

"Thank you," Joanna responded and within a few minutes, Ina had exited through the back door by herself.

Sitting next to Jake in the small country church felt strangely familiar to Joanna, as if they'd been there many times together. Déjà vu, in the truest sense of the word, she mused. Several members of the congregation knew Jake, either from the office or because they were distant neighbors. He shook hands with many of them.

"You fit in as though you belong here," Joanna whispered to him just before the service began. She paged through their small, worn hymnal to the opening song. Then she worried if she'd said the wrong thing again. But her concern proved to be short-lived when Jake responded positively.

"I've never been here before, but these people make me feel like part of them."

The message Pastor White gave that morning was exceptionally good, and when the invitation was given for people to come forward to the altar, the young woman sitting next to Ina in the choir loft responded. Ina and several other members of the congregation went to the altar to pray with their friend.

Joanna bowed her head to pray where she sat in the pew, but was accustomed to going up front to pray with someone when they went forward. She hesitated, not sure if she should leave Jake's side on his first visit to the church. Then she decided his presence probably shouldn't change her actions. She rose from her seat and joined several members of her church family at the polished oak kneeling rail at the front of the sanctuary.

After the time of prayer, the service concluded. Joanna looked back toward her seat, only to discover Jake no longer there. Scanning the small crowd of people mingling here and there, greeting one another, she spotted him off to one side of the sanctuary. He was speaking with Pastor White.

Ina swished by in her gold choir robe and squeezed Joanna's arm. She nodded her head toward Jake and the pastor. "He's talking to the right man."

Joanna smiled in return and watched Ina disappear into the choir room. Picking up her Bible and purse, she walked toward the men.

Jake gave an easy smile when he saw her approaching. He hadn't thought of how pretty she looked more than a time or two that morning. His mind had been on more serious matters, but with her walking toward him now he couldn't escape it. Joanna was lovely, alive with a sense of life he'd either lost touch with or never known. He wasn't sure which.

"So, you're getting to know Pastor White," she said.

"Yes, we're getting acquainted," the minister confirmed. "I was just telling Dr. Barnes that I teach a men's Sunday School class, and I'd really like for him to join us this morning."

"Jake, that would be perfect," Joanna suggested. "I'm helping with one of the children's classes, so I'll be busy."

"It does sound interesting, Pastor. I'd be happy to join you."

Joanna whispered a silent thank you to the Lord as she walked down the long, narrow hallway toward the Sunday School rooms with the two men. Having Jake come to church this morning was a very pleasant surprise, but his interest in Sunday School bordered on miraculous.

Joanna went to the children's classroom she had offered to help with and was greeted by a half-dozen rowdy four-year-olds. By the time she had made it through the story of Daniel in the lions' den, the meaning was nearly lost in the midst of the children's interest in becoming little lion cubs themselves. And the animal crackers Joanna served for snack only encouraged their newfound activity. Finally, she decided to get on the floor and join them, remembering the old adage "if you can't beat 'em, join 'em." It actually helped, she discovered. As the "mother" lion she was able to round the kids into a circle and have them sing a couple of their favorite Bible songs before the final bell rang for dismissal. Joanna was picking up toppled chairs and cookie crumbs when Jake walked into the room.

"How did it go with the kids?" he asked.

"It could have been better," she replied, pushing the last tiny chair back into its proper place. "But I think they all had a good time." Jake had always seemed tall to Joanna, but never so much as now when he stood in the doorway of a room filled with miniature furniture.

"I have your coat, if you're ready to go." He held it open for her while she slipped her arms into the silky sleeves. When she turned toward him, Jake reached for the crooked collar to straighten it. After doing so, he stood still for a moment with his hands on the collar, looking into her face. Not saying a word.

Joanna glanced down at the strong hands that remained on her coat, then she returned her uncertain gaze to his.

In that instant, Jake was forced to face a fact he'd run from for months, if not years. He wanted this woman. In every way. He wanted to protect her, hold her, walk beside her through life. He wanted to be the man to help her with her coat and listen to her stories about Sunday School or her work at Smithfield. The harder he tried to ignore it, the stronger that feeling became. And Jake was growing weary of the struggle.

Joanna watched a look of despair pass over his features before he pulled his hands away.

"Sorry," was all he said, and he nodded toward the exit. But then much to Joanna's surprise, he reached for her hand, clasping it in his while they headed toward the car.

"How was Sunday School?" she asked, trying not

to let her voice betray how important the matter was to her.

"Interesting," Jake replied. "Very interesting."

Joanna tried in every subtle way she could think of to find out exactly what Jake thought of the service and the Sunday School class as they drove home, but to no avail. He didn't seem willing to discuss the specifics, and she did not want to appear too nosy, so their conversation drifted to other areas. Including the fact that Joanna had only an hour and a half before she had to be at Smithfield for her afternoon shift.

She had time for a quick lunch, which she ate upstairs with her aunt. Mae was awake, sitting in a chair by the window and very talkative for which Joanna was grateful. She promised her aunt she'd visit with her more when she came home from work later in the day. Then she slipped into jeans and a T-shirt and headed for work. Anything she was going to find out from Jake about his views on Christianity, would have to wait until another day.

Work and visiting with Aunt Mae kept Joanna occupied during the following days. Mae was well enough to want to come downstairs for dinner one evening, against the wishes of the nurse on duty. Since Jake wasn't home to okay the idea, Ina and Joanna agreed not to attempt it. Instead they carried the meal up to her room to enjoy a time together there, and Joanna began to think about returning home. Aunt Mae's improving condition put that goal within sight.

Then the weather turned surprisingly pleasant and sunny for Indiana in early March.

Joanna brought Aaron home from Smithfield with her one warm evening, and they were standing outside on the patio when Jake came home from the office. The grill was going. Joanna was placing large, thick hamburgers on it and Aaron was helping himself to the dill pickles Ina had placed on the picnic table. The double glass doors slid open, and Jake stepped out onto the patio.

"Hi," Joanna said and smiled at him, watching him loosen his burgundy print tie. "You don't care much for neckties, do you?" she added. He frequently seemed to be taking one off.

Jake grinned. "No, I don't." He surveyed the grill, the picnic table and the redheaded child. "We're having a cookout? In March?"

"Yes, it's nearly seventy degrees out here." Joanna turned the hamburger patties on the grill. "And we have company tonight." She noticed Aaron scooting closer to her and finally taking a seat on the picnic table, while studying Jake cautiously.

"So I see," Jake answered as he smiled at the youngster. He dropped his tie and jacket into a nearby lawn chair. "Let's see...red hair and handsome green eyes. You must be Aaron."

Joanna could recall describing the boy to Jake only once. She was pleased he remembered.

"How'd you know me?" Aaron asked quickly, and he stood up, mystified by Jake's accuracy.

"Well, for one thing, I'm the doctor that comes to Smithfield every Wednesday to see whichever of you guys is sick, although I didn't see you there this week. I know you because Miss Meccord has told me a lot about you,'' Jake explained as he rolled up the long sleeves of his white shirt.

Joanna was irritated with herself for watching his movements so closely. She'd barely seen him all week and had missed him far more than she wanted to admit. Reaching for the wet cloth on the table, she wiped her hands, glad for an excuse to look away.

Aaron was standing now, studying Jake's six-foot frame intently. "Miss Meccord told you?" His freckled nose wrinkled up in a frown. It was obvious he'd never heard Joanna addressed so formally. "You mean Jo-Jo?"

"Yes." Jake's broad smile lit up his face, and his eyes flickered over her in amusement. "I meant Jo-Jo."

Joanna laughed softly at the sound of Jake's voice repeating her nickname, and she focused on the hamburger platter she was picking up rather than meet his silver-gray gaze. Carrying the plate to the grill, she placed several burgers on it.

"Aaron," she began, realizing she had not properly introduced Jake to their guest. "This is Dr. Barnes. I've told you about him." Glancing again at the child, she saw that he'd edged a few inches from the picnic bench, moving a little closer to Jake while still maintaining his distance.

"You're a doctor? You give people shots and stuff?" Aaron asked, frowning intensely at the unpleasant thought.

"Sometimes I do," Jake answered as he approached the boy and crouched down to eye level with him, "but I'm not planning to give any tonight." Jake held out his arm, and Aaron placed his small hand slowly into Jake's to receive a hearty handshake. "I'm glad you could join us for dinner, Aaron."

"Oh, I'm not just here for dinner. I'm here for the night," came Aaron's prompt response.

Joanna froze, spatula in midair. She had not had an opportunity to ask Jake about bringing Aaron here with her. The situation had come up so suddenly that she had made the decision without his approval. This certainly wasn't the way she had planned to break the news to him. "Surprise," she said weakly, casting an apologetic look in his direction.

He had to be surprised by the announcement, but she couldn't see it in his expression and Joanna was grateful. With a smile, he assured Aaron they'd have a good time while he was there. "I'll bet you like to play baseball."

"Yes, sir, I do!" Aaron exclaimed, once again amazed by Jake's knowledge about him. A lucky guess, Jake would have gladly admitted. "I'll go get my ball and glove," the boy said. "I brought 'em with me, just in case!" He ran across the patio, opened the sliding doors and disappeared inside the house.

Carefully, Joanna lifted another hamburger from the grill, then looked up to see Jake standing, one hand sunk into the pocket of his dark slacks and the other rubbing the back of his neck. He stood staring into the doorway through which Aaron had run.

"Did you have a hard day?" Joanna asked, watching him turn to face her.

"It was hectic, but I still managed to get out earlier than expected." He walked toward her to inspect her cooking.

"We can eat in just a few minutes," she said and hesitated. "Jake, I hope you don't mind my bringing Aaron home for the night. The person he was scheduled to go away with canceled at the last minute. He was crying his eyes out, and I couldn't stand it...so I invited him to come with me." She turned back to the grill to check the remaining hamburgers. "I promise to keep him entertained so he won't be in your way. And we brought his sleeping bag, so he can sleep in my room."

"That's fine," Jake said quietly. He was standing behind her, looking over her shoulder at the meat on the grill. As she talked, he placed his hands on her shoulders in a familiarity he rarely exhibited.

The warmth of his unexpected touch distracted her so, she could barely remember what she'd been rambling on about. Aaron, she recalled. "I—I didn't have a chance to check with you first. I didn't think you'd mind having him here overnight, but I realize this is your home—"

"It's alright, Jo-Jo," Jake responded. "It's no problem."

Without even turning to face him, she could sense he was smiling. She went on, "I realize I should have cleared this with you first, but I didn't have time to call. I don't want to overstep my boundaries or make you angry." She stopped talking, suddenly realizing that he really didn't seem to have any objections. "And why are you calling me Jo-Jo?"

"Having Aaron around is fine with me, and I think Jo-Jo is a good name for you." His easy laugh flowed over her and he squeezed her shoulders before walking away. He casually reached across the table into a bowl of potato chips, taking a few. "What would I have to be angry with you for? Cluttering up my life with a needy child and a beautiful woman?"

Joanna stared at him. "Meaning…what?" she asked as she turned to join him beside the table. Had he just told her she was beautiful, or was she imagining things?

"Meaning…" he began, the corners of his mouth easing down as the smile disappeared and a stillness entered his voice. "I'll miss that…I'll miss you, when you go."

Almost without thinking, she responded, "I know," in little more than a whisper. "Me, too." And then, just for a moment, she thought he might kiss her. Their eyes locked in some unexplainable battle, stormy gray blazing into misty brown. That night by the fireplace—the tenderness, the longing—did not seem so out of reach.

Then the patio door flew open, offering the arrival of Aaron, ball and glove in hand and Ina carrying a huge bowl of potato salad.

"Time to eat!" Ina announced, placing the bowl on the table. She poured fresh iced tea for everyone. Then Joanna said the blessing and the meal got underway.

Later than evening, Jake and Joanna both tossed

the ball back and forth with Aaron, and the disturbing moment they had shared earlier seemed a million miles away. It wasn't long until Aaron felt quite at home with them and by the end of the evening had acquired the nickname champ, which seemed to please him greatly. Eventually, even Ina joined in the activities throwing an easy pitch or two.

After Joanna had tucked Aaron into his sleeping bag for the night and he had actually gone to sleep, she returned to the backyard.

"Relaxing in a lawn chair? In March?" she teased when she found Jake sitting outside.

"Somebody told me it was nearly seventy degrees today," he replied and motioned to the empty chair next to him. "Have a seat."

"Thank you for playing with Aaron," she said softly, sitting down as she spoke. She stared up at the stars on this unseasonably warm evening. "He really came to life around you. You're good for him."

"We both had a good time. He's a great kid, Jo." He leaned back with his hands folded behind his head.

"I didn't realize until tonight how much he needs the attention of a man," Joanna spoke her private thoughts aloud.

Jake looked up at the velvety black sky. "Doesn't he have much contact with any of the men at Smithfield? There are quite a few on staff."

"I know, but Aaron's living unit has mostly women right now. There's really only Bob. He spends as much time with him as he can."

"Who's Bob?" Jake asked. "I don't remember meeting him there."

"He's one of the staff members assigned to Aaron's group. I think he's usually off on Wednesdays. That's probably why you don't know him."

A few moments of silence followed, and Joanna folded her arms together, hugging them to her stomach to fight the sudden invading chill of dropping temperatures.

"Here," Jake offered as he reached into a nearby chair to retrieve the jacket he'd dropped there earlier. He leaned forward to hand it to her.

"Thank you," she answered, slipping the jacket around her shoulders with some hesitation. She knew how it would feel beneath the weight of his coat. Warm. Safe. And the faint scent of his cologne filled her senses with the memory of being in his arms.

"Better?" he asked quietly while watching her through narrowing eyes.

Joanna's heart thumped noisily in response to the tension he created in her as he reached toward her again. The fingers that brushed her ear were cool as Jake tucked away strands of blond hair, but she didn't mind. His lingering touch was exactly what she needed. There was far more between them than friendship. She'd seen it, felt it. So had he.

But Jake pulled his hand away in an achingly slow movement and transferred his gaze out into the darkness that surrounded them.

"Jake?" she said softly.

"It's getting colder," he responded, disregarding her one-word question. "It's starting to feel more like March."

They walked into the house together in silence.

Hand in hand. But Joanna didn't say any more than good-night to him. The moment had come and gone again. But, maybe, if she was patient and if the Lord allowed, it would return. And remain.

Chapter Seven

"Joanna, could you arrange to be off Thursday this week?" Jake asked.

"I think so," she replied. "Why?"

"I'm not going to work that day. Do you think Aaron would be interested in spending it with us?" Jake placed the morning newspaper on the coffee table.

Us. She hadn't heard him use that word lately. It had a nice, but rare sound to it. "I'm sure he'd love to. I'll ask the group supervisor if she'll approve it."

"Can you take care of it today?"

"Yes, I'll check into it," she answered, watching him straighten the knot of his gray tie in the living room mirror. "But it might be more special for Aaron if you took him by yourself. He's too used to having me around."

"No, I want you to come." Their eyes met in the reflection of the glass. "How about the zoo?" he asked.

"That would be fine. He'll enjoy being with you no matter where you take him."

"Maybe the zoo in the afternoon, and then we'll take him to Gallery Lane," Jake said. He picked up his jacket and headed for the front door.

"Gallery Lane?" Joanna repeated.

"It's a mall with restaurants and shops not far from the zoo. Haven't you been there?"

"No, I've never heard of it."

"Then Ina's not doing a very good job showing you around this area," he said with one corner of his mouth lifting into a grin. "We'll try to correct that. I'll see you later."

"Bye," she called after him and watched him walk out toward his car. Then she closed the door. A day with Jake and Aaron? That could be wonderful. On the other hand, it could also shatter what was left of her heart into a thousand piercing pieces. She gave a soft sigh and headed toward the kitchen.

"Is Dr. Barnes gone?" Ina asked at first sight of Joanna.

"Yes, Ina, he just left." She began to help clear away the breakfast dishes.

"I wish you wouldn't do that," Ina said. "That's what I get paid to do around here. Be a housekeeper. Remember?"

"I don't need to be at work for an hour, and the nurse doesn't want me up there with Aunt Mae right now because she's sleeping. I may as well help you."

But Ina was still frowning. "Did you know that Jake had a phone call this morning from a Dr. Karen Kingsley? She said she was a friend of his."

Joanna placed some cups in the sink. Karen Kingsley? The name sounded vaguely familiar. Maybe she'd been one of the doctors who had volunteered occasionally at the clinic?

"She's coming for a visit. They sounded very friendly on the phone, Joanna. He seemed glad she called."

Joanna's smile was sweet but sad. "It's okay, Ina. You don't need to protect me from anything. Jake is entitled to his friends, girlfriends...whatever. He doesn't belong to me. He never did." She picked up the orange juice and margarine to put them into the refrigerator.

"What we need around here is a little honesty. If you don't tell him how you feel about him, I'm going to."

"Don't you dare!" Joanna returned with a startled look. "You'd embarrass me half to death, Ina. Jake knows enough about my feelings."

"But if you'd try a little harder—"

"I'm not going to *try* anything," Joanna defended quickly. "I'm not beautiful, brilliant or particularly successful at anything, and I'm not going to pretend. Jake will either love me some day the way I am, or he'll never love me at all. That's all there is to it."

"Oh, please. I don't think you've revealed a nickel's worth of your feelings. I'm not saying you need to pretend you're something you're not. But I don't think either one of you is a bit truthful with yourselves or each other, and if you can't have a little honesty, then you won't have anything."

The silverware tumbled noisily into the sink. "He's

taking Thursday off this week, and we're going to spend the day with Aaron.'' Joanna tried a change of subject. "I think we're going to the zoo.''

"Tell him how you feel. Here at home, Thursday at the zoo, today at his office. Somewhere. Sometime!''

"I can't,'' Joanna replied sharply. "Neither one of us would know what to say next, Ina. He'd just reiterate to me that it would never work. That night of the blizzard, he made it clear that he'd never...''

"Never what?''

"Never have anything to offer me. Nothing lasting, nothing beyond friendship,'' she answered quietly. How could those words hurt so much now? This was something she'd faced squarely. And almost accepted. Hadn't she? "And I respect that friendship enough to leave bad enough alone—if you know what I mean.''

"But Joanna—''

"I love him, Ina, but Jake was my friend before things took a romantic turn. If I tell him something he doesn't want to hear, it will only ruin what we already have. And I won't risk that.'' She couldn't risk that. It meant too much.

"Try anyway, Aaron. It's a long drive to the zoo,'' Joanna said as she picked up the small red jacket from the foot of the boy's bed. The room Aaron shared with Freddie was tiny but brightly painted with vivid blues and yellows, and balloons cut from red felt hung on one wall—not unlike a room Joanna had known as a child.

"Ready, Jo-Jo!'' Aaron came rushing out of the

bathroom and reached for the baseball cap on top of his dresser. "Let's go!"

Aaron raced ahead of her, rushing through the doorway into the living area. "Where's Doc?" He looked around the empty room.

"He's at the front desk picking up your medical card," Joanna answered.

"What's that?"

Joanna handed the jacket to Aaron as she explained, "It's a piece of paper that gives us permission to take you to a hospital if you're not feeling well while you're with us."

"But I feel okay," Aaron assured her, "and anyways, I won't need no hospital. I've got Doc with me."

Joanna gave a soft laugh as they walked through the activity area toward the front office. Smithfield was quiet this Thursday afternoon. Most of the children were away on field trips, and the ones who had stayed behind were involved in arts and crafts activities in the recreation center.

"Doc!" Aaron shouted when he neared the front office and caught sight of Jake standing in the lobby.

"Aaron, honey, this is an office where people are working, so we need to be kind of quiet," Joanna said softly, tugging on his baseball cap and pulling it down on his forehead.

"Jo-Jo, don't!" Aaron said, but he was laughing even as he protested.

Joanna opened the heavy glass door to the front office, and Aaron hurried inside. But a shyness came over him, which Joanna had seen settle over him before. He stood several feet away from Jake, looking up at him through apprehensive green eyes.

"Hi, champ," Jake said, coaxing a smile from the freckled-face boy standing awkwardly in front of him. "No hug for me, huh?" Jake knelt down, and Aaron rushed toward him, wrapping his little arms around Jake's neck. "Now that's what I call a hug. Are you ready to go, champ?"

"I was born ready!" Aaron exclaimed as he released his grip on Jake. He pushed hard against the glass office door, but it was so heavy he barely budged it.

"Here, I'll get it." Jake pushed the door open with one hand. "Better save your energy for the zoo."

Aaron raced ahead of them toward Jake's automobile, which was parked in front of the building.

"I guess we're the ones who should be conserving our energy, if we're going to keep up with him all day," Jake commented quietly to Joanna as they watched Aaron pull open the car door.

"You ought to try taking fifteen of them somewhere," Joanna remarked.

Jake laughed. "I like kids, Jo, but I have no self-destructive tendencies."

She smiled and tipped her face to the sun. "It's a beautiful day."

"Perfect," Jake commented and inclined his head toward the car. "Shall we?"

Her smile widened. "Let's go."

"How long till we get there?" Aaron called out to them, his enthusiasm evident in every syllable of his speech.

"About half an hour," Jake answered.

"Hello, Barb," Joanna called to the small, dark-haired young woman who was walking toward them from the parking lot.

"You're not working today, are you?" Barbara asked as she neared them.

"No, we're picking up Aaron for the day. We're going to the zoo. Barbara, this is Dr. Jake Barnes. I think you've met him—"

"No, actually, I haven't," she said and extended an arm for a handshake. "I'm off on Wednesdays, so I'm not here when you are, Dr. Barnes. It's good to meet you."

"Nice to meet you, Barbara," Jake responded, and then turned his attention to Aaron who had come running back to Jake and stood tugging his arm.

"There's Freddie comin' back with his volunteer. Can we talk to him before we go? Can we?" Aaron pleaded.

"I don't see why not," Jake answered, glancing at Joanna for her reaction.

"That's fine," she replied, waving at Freddie who was across the parking lot from them.

"Excuse us, ladies," Jake said, and the two of them walked toward the car that had just pulled into the parking lot.

"It's nice to finally meet him," Barbara remarked as she and Joanna watched them walk away. "But, wow!" she added. "I see now why so many eyebrows shot up when you said you were living with Dr. Barnes."

"Barbara, please keep your voice down."

"You say you're sort of renting a room from him?"

"No, not exactly. I'm just staying in his house until my aunt is well enough to return home. It's going to be quite a while before I can afford to start repaying him."

"I can think of ways to—"

"Barb," Joanna said sharply, bringing an abrupt end to the statement. "There's nothing going on between us."

Barbara looked at Joanna in bewilderment. "Are you really serious? There's nothing going on between you and this great-looking guy you're living with?"

"The only thing going on is that we're taking Aaron to the zoo together," Joanna assured her.

Barbara glanced from Joanna to Jake. "If you say so...," she remarked as she walked away.

"I think we're ready," Jake said to Joanna as he opened her car door. Aaron bounded into the back seat.

"Freddie thinks this is a neat car, too," Aaron commented when Jake started the engine, and they were on their way.

Nearly thirty minutes, much conversation and lots of laughter had passed by the time they pulled into the zoo parking lot.

"Okay. Rule number one is, you must stay with us," Joanna stated.

"Do I hafta hold your hand all day?" Aaron groaned.

"No, but I don't want you out of my sight. Understood?"

"Yes, ma'am," came Aaron's reply.

"If you break that rule, then we'll have to hold hands."

Jake laughed quietly, drawing Joanna's attention his direction. "Punishment I think I could withstand," he said, his quick gray eyes filled with humor. He reached across the seat to squeeze Joanna's hand.

She had to look away. Her stomach had that silly fluttering feeling in it again. Schoolgirlish stuff, she thought. Something she didn't want to deal with today. "Rule number two, Aaron—keep your hands away from all cages. I don't want you to get hurt."

"But, Jo-Jo, I just want to—"

"No arguments. Hands off the cages."

"Okay, okay," Aaron reluctantly agreed. "No argument from me 'cause you're a real good arguer."

"I know she is," Jake commented, still smiling. "I argued with her about moving here."

"And you won?" Aaron asked.

"I won," Jake replied.

"Did you kiss and make up?"

"Aaron," Joanna said firmly as she clamped a hand lightly over his mouth. "That's enough." Her face grew warm despite the cool temperature.

"Did you?" Aaron persisted, the words barely distinguishable beneath Joanna's palm.

"No," Jake answered. "Not then."

Joanna flashed a disapproving look in Jake's direction, releasing Aaron as she did so. "We weren't really angry with each other, Aaron."

"We rarely are," Jake acknowledged quietly. "Are we?"

"No," she admitted, her pulse skittering.

"Let's go!" Aaron insisted. He climbed up front to get out of the car, so Joanna opened her door.

It was a cool but sunny day in March, and they spent several hours looking at giraffes, gazelles and gorillas galore, lions and rhinos, monkeys and bears and animals Aaron had never heard of. Joanna had a small disposable camera that she had purchased for Aaron. He took lots of pictures of his favorite animals.

"Look! We can pet those," Aaron exclaimed when he saw the children's zoo. "Can't we?" He looked up at Joanna.

"Sure can," she replied as she pulled change from the pocket of her red-floral-print skirt and dropped a coin into the feeder. "Put your hand under here," she instructed him, and when she turned the metal dial, tiny food pellets filled the child's hands. "Go ahead, you can feed them. They won't hurt you," she said, looking toward the small goats that had crowded by the gate. Aaron walked into the midst of the greedy crowd and sprinkled a few pellets on the ground quickly rather than allowing them to eat from his hand.

Jake and Joanna stood leaning against the heavy wooden rail fencing. They watched Aaron move hesitantly through the flock of animals all clamoring for his attention and a bite of the food he held tightly in his small fists.

"You're surrounded, Aaron. I think that means it's time to surrender," Jake suggested.

"That's worse than walking into Smithfield with a

candy bar in your possession,'' Joanna commented with a light laugh.

Aaron tossed the remaining pellets into the air and came scrambling out of the fenced area toward the railing where they were waiting.

"Didn't you enjoy that?" Joanna asked quickly, noticing the frown on his face.

"Yep," he said, adjusting his ball cap. "But I need more of that stuff they like."

"Okay, champ," Jake replied, and he pulled a couple of quarters from his pocket. "Here you go."

Aaron took off his hat, letting the pellets from the machine fall into it; and he was soon back in the midst of the petting zoo, laughing and enjoying himself with the other children that had joined him.

"I suppose he'd do that all day, if we let him," Jake said, observing Aaron's happy antics.

"Until we ran out of quarters," Joanna confirmed.

"Do you think a hamburger and a chocolate shake would entice him away from here? I haven't had any lunch."

"It's nearly five o'clock," Joanna responded. "Aaron, honey, come on. Let's go," she called out and then turned to Jake. "You shouldn't skip meals, Jake. You must be starving."

He laughed quietly at her statement, and Aaron came running up to him. Leaning over, he picked up the boy. "You're beginning to sound like Carmen. She's usually the one who lectures me about skipping lunch."

"Who's Carmen?" Joanna asked immediately.

That was a name she couldn't recall hearing him mention.

"Our receptionist at the office. The one you didn't like very much," he managed to say without smiling, but Joanna had the feeling it required a lot of effort to do so.

"Oh, yes." How could she forget? "The one with the gorgeous Pacific-blue eyes."

"They're blue, are they?" He avoided her gaze as they walked toward the zoo exit, and she knew it was deliberate.

"Jake, be serious. They're the bluest eyes I've ever seen. You had to notice them when you hired her," she said. That among other things, Joanna thought to herself. Carmen was an incredibly attractive woman. Then a thought occurred to her. Maybe those extraordinary eyes were the result of colored contact lenses. Not that it mattered much. Everything else looked very real.

"You'll have to blame Andrew for Carmen's presence in that office. He's the one who hired her, crime that it was." And this time, Jake's mouth did give way to a smile. A wide one. He looked her way. "C'mon, let's go eat. I am starving."

"I don't suppose you could fire her on the basis of being too distracting to work around," Joanna remarked as she kept pace with Jake's stride.

"I don't think so," he answered after stalling for a moment as though he were considering the possibility. "She does a pretty fair job at the front desk, and she's pleasant enough, considering she's a person with no discernible sense of humor."

That made Joanna smile. "See, I knew I'd find a flaw in there somewhere." She slipped her arm through Jake's. "No one's *that* perfect. Let's go eat. Now I'm starving, too." She shifted her attention to Aaron. "Did you have fun today, hon?"

"It was cool! This zoo is the funnest one I've ever been to. There's more stuff here than any other."

Jake said, "Now that your animal friends are well fed, how about you? Are you hungry yet?"

"Yes, I'm hungry," he answered and then wriggled from Jake's arms to walk beside them. "Can I take my jacket off, Jo-Jo?"

"No, hon, you'd better leave it on." She touched his forehead, feeling a slight dampness of the hair at his temples. "I don't want you to catch cold."

"I wanna hamburger and some fries with lotsa ketchup," Aaron requested.

"I think what you mean is lots of ketchup with a few fries," she said with a light laugh. "I've seen you eat French fries."

"Either way, we'll find what you want, champ. Just stick with us," Jake assured him as they walked toward the car.

"Hamburger with what?" Jake asked when they stood at the counter in one of the many small restaurants that lined the Gallery.

"Pickles, ketchup, mustard," Aaron rattled off the items as though he'd placed that order numerous times, "and large fries."

"With ketchup," he and Jake said simultaneously.

"And I want white soda to drink," Aaron added, fiddling with the straw dispenser.

"It's clear, Aaron. Not white," Joanna remarked, removing the half-dozen straws Aaron had in his hands and placing them on the counter.

"Clear as opposed to brown," Joanna said with a smile in response to Jake's glance her direction.

"Okay," Jake said. "What about you? There are dozens of things to choose from. You don't really want a hamburger, do you?"

"No, I'd rather look around," she answered.

After they had purchased Aaron's meal, they found a place to sit at one of small round tables in the center of the Gallery.

Joanna opened a couple of ketchup packets for Aaron to prevent it from being squirted everywhere. "There are so many restaurants here, Jake." She did not really know what she wanted to try. "What do you like the looks of?" She glanced up in question to his lack of response, only to find he was looking directly at her. Some undefinable emotion darkened his eyes, his expression.

"What's wrong?" she asked softly.

Just then, Aaron bit into his sandwich. "Mmm..."

Jake shook his head. "Nothing," he responded. "What would you like for dinner?"

Food was the last thing on Joanna's mind as she sat looking up at him, wondering what troubled him so. There was a deli behind where Jake was standing, and the colorful red-white-and-blue sign caught her attention. "How about a sub?" She motioned toward the nearest shop.

"That sounds good," he said, glancing at the restaurant. "What do you want to drink? Clear soda, too?"

"No, thanks. I'd prefer lemonade if they have it."

He was smiling, but he was not happy, and Joanna wished she could understand why.

The subs served on warm homemade bread tasted delicious. And for dessert, they enjoyed hot fudge sundaes while Aaron worked his way through the large vanilla ice cream cone he'd requested.

After they'd browsed through practically every shop on the premises, Joanna purchased a half-dozen peanut butter cookies from one of the bakeries for Aaron to take back to Smithfield with him. Then it was time to leave.

"Not yet!" Aaron protested loudly as they started the drive toward home.

"Sorry, honey, but you need to get home to get ready for bed. It's getting late," Joanna explained.

"We'll spend another day together soon, Aaron," Jake added.

"Promise?"

Jake glanced in the rearview mirror, seeing Aaron's hopeful expression. "I promise."

Aaron was silent for a moment before asking, "And you keep your promises?"

"I do," Jake said solemnly.

The reply seemed to satisfy Aaron because in a matter of minutes, he was curled up in one corner of the back seat, sound asleep.

"He had a wonderful time, Jake," Joanna commented softly while they drove down the highway. She glanced back at the sleeping boy.

"I hope he did."

"I *know* he did," Joanna confirmed. She folded her hands together in front of her, resisting the urge to touch the hand that rested on the gearshift near her leg.

Jake nodded, but he said nothing as he guided the car onto the next exit ramp.

Having Aaron walk into Smithfield was impossible, so Jake gathered up the groggy boy in his arms, carrying him inside the building.

"You've got a sleepy one on your hands, I see," Barbara remarked when they entered Aaron's living area.

"He's had a big day," Joanna explained.

Jake placed the child on his narrow twin bed, and Joanna handed the cookies over to her co-worker.

"Here, Barb, you'd better put these in the office. If Freddie gets into them, there will be war."

"I'll take care of him from here, Joanna. Go on home," Barbara said. "And have a great evening," she added with a suggestive lift of one eyebrow in Joanna's direction when Jake wasn't looking.

"See you in the morning," Joanna replied with a quick frown, and within minutes she and Jake were in the car again.

"It went well, don't you think?" he asked.

Joanna stared out the window into the darkness. "Yes, Aaron loved it...and so did I, Jake." She tilted her head to see his reaction. "Thank you for planning this."

"My pleasure," Jake responded without taking his eyes off the road.

Leaning her head back, she relaxed against the headrest and closed her eyes as they rode along in silence—the comfortable silence she'd grown accustomed to sharing with him.

"How was the zoo?" Ina greeted them at the front door in her housecoat and fuzzy slippers.

"We had a wonderful time," Joanna said. "Aaron really enjoyed himself. We all did. And Gallery Lane is marvelous, Ina. So much food, so little time." She gave her friend a hug.

"That's great," Ina enthused. "There's a fresh pot of coffee and a German chocolate cake in the kitchen if you have any room left for dessert."

"I'll have coffee," Joanna said and she walked toward the kitchen. "Jake?" she looked back over her shoulder at him. "Would you like something?"

"No, thank you," he replied, picking up the mail stacked by the telephone. "I have a few things to take care of."

"Well, I'm going upstairs to see how Mae's doing," Ina remarked. "Maybe she'd be interested in a bite of cake. And that nurse, too. What's this one's name?" she asked with a frown as she headed up the staircase.

"I'm not sure," Jake said. "I didn't meet her when she came in this morning. Good night, Ina."

"Good night," she answered.

Joanna soon came out of the kitchen with a cup of black coffee in her hands. "I'm going to tell Aunt

Mae about our day, and then I have some studying to do," she commented. She saw that Jake was thumbing through mail and still had a stack of telephone messages waiting for him as she started up the staircase.

"What are you studying?" he asked without looking up.

"It's for church. We're reading Galatians," she answered before taking a sip of coffee.

"Living by faith, not the law," Jake stated.

Joanna choked on the coffee she was swallowing, coughing hard.

"Are you okay?" he asked, staring up at her where she stood about halfway up the staircase.

"Yes," she said with difficulty, coughing again. "How did you know that?"

"Know what?" His mouth quirked with humor as he placed the mail on a small table nearby.

"About Galatians!" she exclaimed. "How did you know?"

"I read it," he responded, his mouth giving way to a generous smile. "You told me a few things about Ephesians one night before you left for church, so I decided to do some reading on my own."

"That's...wonderful," she stammered, "that's amazing. I'm just so surprised."

"Obviously," Jake agreed with a quiet laugh and reached for the phone messages.

Then Joanna remembered Bible study. "Maybe you'd like to come with me on Wednesday night. Pastor White is the teacher."

"I can't this week, Jo. There's a meeting at the

hospital that I need to attend, but I will go with you sometime.''

"Promise?" she echoed Aaron's word.

"I'm being asked to make a lot of promises to-day," Jake said when he looked back into her shining eyes—dark, gentle eyes he could spend the rest of his life looking into. "Yes, I promise."

"And you keep your promises?" She saw his smile fade.

"I do," Jake answered. He thought of marriage vows and broken hearts as he watched her turn and continue up the stairs. Joanna opened the door to her bedroom, smiling down at him before she disappeared inside.

Then Jake quietly asked the real question that stood between them. The one that only time would answer.

"Do you?"

Chapter Eight

"Come on, Aaron," Joanna called out to the young boy as she grabbed up her purse and jacket. "Let's go get some dinner. Your caseworker said it would be all right for you to spend some extra time with me this week."

That was a direct answer to her recent prayers. Spending time with Aaron was something she not only enjoyed, but felt strongly she should do. He'd had so little attention paid to him by anybody, ever, as far as Joanna could tell. She couldn't undo the past, but she could provide some special times for him now, as long as she worked there.

They were soon in her car, discussing the events of the day including Freddie's run-away attempt. He'd been found hiding in the back of the van that had just returned from a field trip. He'd stayed on board after everyone else went in, hoping to slip out unnoticed and head for the shopping strip within walking distance of Smithfield. He had a pocket full of money and big plans of how to spend it when Barbara discovered him underneath one of the back seats.

Aaron said he'd never run away, which Joanna believed. Aaron wasn't nearly as adventurous as Freddie was proving to be for which everyone on staff was grateful.

After arriving at Jake's house, they entered through the front doorway. There was a light on in Jake's study, but Joanna peeked in, and it was empty. Ina had the day off, so she wasn't expected back any time soon. "We'll go up and visit with Aunt Mae as soon as I fix something to eat," she told Aaron.

Then laughter, high and unfamiliar, floated through the air. It was coming from the living room.

"Is that Ina?" Aaron asked.

"No," Joanna answered. It certainly wasn't Ina. It didn't sound like anyone she knew. Maybe Jake had a visitor. "Let's go into the kitchen. I'm doing the cooking tonight."

"Can you cook hot dogs? That's one thing I like. Or macaroni and cheese?"

"Yes," Joanna told him. "I can cook all that and more, believe it or not."

The clock on the wall caught Joanna's eye. She had thought Jake would be home by now, but she also knew he wasn't expecting her until much later that evening. She'd traded shifts unexpectedly with Barbara to help out her friend. Joanna had not thought of letting Jake know, but she was wishing now that she had. This could be embarrassing. For all of them.

The laughter started again. Charming. Light. And the way to the kitchen was through the living room.

As she neared the room, she saw an attractive brunette seated on the sofa, leaning close to Jake as they looked at the photo album before them on the coffee table. Joanna saw only the brunette while Aaron noticed only Jake.

"Hi, Doc!" the child exclaimed, but remained close by Joanna.

They should have left without disturbing them, Joanna thought. She wished now they'd gone out for pizza. Tacos. Anything.

"Champ! How ya doin'?" Jake asked, smiling at the boy. He stood up and so did the lovely lady with him. "Jo, I'm glad you're here."

Joanna doubted his statement, but thought it kind of him to pretend rather than make her feel worse for interrupting them. She attempted a smile.

"I want you to meet Dr. Karen Kingsley," he began. "And, Karen, this is Joanna Meccord."

"It's nice to meet you, Dr. Kingsley," Joanna said politely, shaking the woman's hand.

"Please, call me Karen. It's nice to meet you, too, Joanna. I'm a friend of Jake's from South Carolina. I know him from college and the clinic." Her short, curly crop of hair was quite flattering and another set of sparkling blue eyes greeted Joanna.

Joanna tried to think of something to say. Something other than, "How well do you know him?" "This is Aaron," she offered, placing a hand on the child's shoulder.

"Yes," Jake added. "This young man is a friend of ours who visits occasionally."

"I can visit more now. My caseworker said so," Aaron explained.

The look exchanged between Jake and Joanna was obvious—he had no idea to what Aaron was referring.

"I'll tell you about it later," she responded. "Come on, Aaron. Let's go find something to eat and leave Jake and his guest alone."

"I'm glad to have met you, Joanna," the visitor said.

"Thank you. I'm glad to have met you, too." Joanna made their exit as quickly as she could, steering Aaron into the kitchen and closing the door that divided the rooms.

"Macaroni and cheese?" she asked after taking a quick survey of the freezer. Joanna took out the frozen entree and lifted the lid.

"Sure," he agreed and placed his blue-and-gold ball cap on the table as he climbed onto the tall wooden chair. "But I like mine hot."

"It will be after I put it in the microwave. Do you like applesauce?"

"Nope," came the emphatic reply.

"Joanna…" Jake had stepped into the kitchen, alone. "Karen and I are going out for a while."

"Fine," she answered, focusing her eyes on the microwave. "Have a nice time." She didn't look up until she heard him walk away. Soon the laughter left the house. Pulling the curtain away from the window, she watched Jake's car leave the driveway.

Beep. It was the timer.

"Supper is ready," Aaron said.

"It sure is." Joanna set the table, then heated some corn for them and opened a can of pears for dessert. She poured a glass of milk for Aaron and iced tea for herself.

"Do you think Doc will be back soon?" the boy asked.

"I really don't know, Aaron. Let's eat and then we'll play a game or watch TV together." But she didn't really think Jake would be home soon. Not that it mattered. When he did return, it wouldn't be to see her anyway. No matter how much her heart wanted it. She'd always known there was Natalie Eden to consider, but she'd not thought about other women until Karen Kingsley showed up in the living room today with pictures, laughter and memories from the clinic.

"She's kinda silly."

"Who is?" Joanna asked, suddenly aware of Aaron's statement.

"The new girl at Smithfield."

Aaron was talking about the new admission, and Joanna's mouth turned down in a frown. She'd barely heard the boy's words, and wasn't that the reason she'd brought him here? To listen, to be with him...to pay attention to this child so few people had ever paid attention to. She was as guilty as the others, unless she could forget her own concerns and concentrate on Aaron. Just Aaron.

And so they talked. Then, with Aunt Mae watching from her upstairs window, they pitched a baseball around in the yard until their fingers got too cold to continue. Their return to the kitchen warmed them thoroughly as they enjoyed hot chocolate with marsh-mallows and a visit with Mae before returning Aaron to Smithfield. Then a quick hug and Joanna was on her way home again.

Straightening up the kitchen took only minutes, so soon she was back upstairs with Aunt Mae and the night nurse, drinking tea and talking until Mae fell asleep. Then she went into her own room to read so Jake and Karen Kingsley could have the living room to themselves when they came home. That's the way it should be, she reminded herself when she heard his car pulling into the driveway. It was his house, his life. She tried to concentrate on her Bible study les-son, but she found herself listening for Karen's laugh-ter. It would have been pleasant actually, under other circumstances. Jake had every right to see whomever he wished. Joanna was keenly aware of that fact, but the knowledge of it did not make Karen's presence hurt any less. Joanna had apparently overestimated the value of a day at the zoo and a walk through Gallery Lane.

"Jo?"

She jumped at the unexpected sound of a knock on her bedroom door. She'd been so lost in thought that she had not heard Jake coming up the staircase.

"Yes?" She closed her book.

"Did you take Aaron back?"

"You can come in. It's not locked," she said.

Jake pushed open the door, but remained in the doorway. "You took Aaron back already?"

"Yes, I dropped him off about an hour ago." She

listened but heard no one else in the house. "And Karen?"

"She's staying with her sister during her visit. I left her there."

Joanna nodded and glanced away. "I'm sorry that Aaron and I walked in on you unannounced. If I'd known you were expecting company, I wouldn't have brought him here."

"It doesn't matter," Jake replied with a dismissive shrug.

But Joanna had the distinct feeling that it did matter. Was that what he'd come up here to say?

"So, Karen is a doctor, too," she commented. "You must have a lot in common." When he failed to respond, she looked back at him to see what had distracted him from their conversation.

Her closet door was slightly ajar as she had left it after reaching in earlier for a book. Jake was staring at the suitcase stored there—one of the pieces of luggage he had given her years ago.

"Jake?"

He raised his gaze from the suitcase, meeting her eyes. "I'm sorry. What were you saying?"

"Karen is a doctor—"

"Yes, a pediatrician," he answered.

"A pediatrician?" Joanna repeated softly. "She works with children and yet she never said one word to Aaron when he was right there in the same room with her?" Then she feared she'd sounded rude. She hadn't intended it that way. "I'm sorry. I didn't mean—"

"It's okay. You're right." Jake nodded his head

and returned his gaze to the luggage. "I noticed that, too," he responded, "among other things."

What things? Good...bad...what? She wanted to ask, even parted her lips to speak, but then decided against it. It was none of her business.

"You don't laugh much anymore," he commented as he slid a hand into the pocket of his tan slacks. "Not like you used to."

Her heart pounded harder when Jake's attention shifted from the empty suitcase to her troubled eyes.

"I do," she replied very softly. "Maybe not as much as Dr. Kingsley, but—"

"No, you don't," he countered, his mouth thinning into a firm line. "Except sometimes when you're with Aaron. That's one reason I enjoy spending time with both of you. Like at the zoo. Because you seem happier then."

Joanna searched the deep gray of his eyes. So much had happened between them. "Things have changed, Jake." Whether they wanted them to or not.

"Some things," he agreed. Silence filled the room until Jake cleared his throat and switched subjects. "Ina called earlier. She won't be home until tomorrow."

"Tomorrow?" Joanna repeated. "When she said she was going to visit her son, I didn't realize she meant overnight."

"She didn't, but two of her grandchildren have the flu, and she wanted to stay over to help take care of them." He paused. "I didn't think you'd mind. Mae and her nurse are here, but if you're not comfortable—"

"No, it's all right," she replied. "I don't mind."

He nodded. "How did you happen to have Aaron with you tonight?"

"I asked the assistant director to let me spend more time with him. The trip to the zoo went so well, Jake, and I'd been praying about the situation. He doesn't have a volunteer or any family to visit, so I asked if I could do more with him. I think the Lord must have softened up Mrs. Southworth's heart because ordinarily, she's not very agreeable."

Jake studied her serious expression. "Is praying something you do often?"

"Yes," she answered. "Every day."

"You talk to God? I mean, in the same way you would speak to another person?"

"Pretty much. I bow my head or—" She stopped, suddenly a little embarrassed by the private nature of the conversation. She had never attempted to explain prayer to anyone. "You probably don't want to hear—"

"Yes, I do. Go on," he replied.

"Well, I usually bow my head or sometimes I kneel, although I don't really think it matters how I pray. All that matters is that I talk to Him."

"And He hears and answers?"

"He does," Joanna responded. "I don't mean audibly, but the answer always comes. Sometimes yes, sometimes no, and occasionally, not yet." She seemed to have had quite a few prayers fall into the latter category recently. "It's not always the answer I hope for."

Jake nodded as if he understood. But he didn't. He

wasn't sure he ever would. Maybe another topic was a good idea.

"I'm glad they are allowing you to spend additional time with Aaron. You're good for him, Jo."

"I hope so. I know he's good for me." She stood up, smoothing a few wrinkles from her jeans. "I really love that little guy."

"I can see that," Jake remarked.

Joanna walked to the door, placing her hand on the doorknob. It was getting late and she was tired…and Aaron wasn't the only person she loved. If she didn't say good-night soon, she might say more than she should to the man who had just spent the evening with the attractive Dr. Kingsley.

But there was one question that had been bothering her. "Bringing Aaron here for visits…I don't have to do that. Are you sure it's okay with you?"

"You know it is," came the answer she hoped to hear. "It's late," Jake added, and then hesitated there in the doorway as though there was something more. "Joanna…Karen asked if you'd be willing to give her a tour of Smithfield."

"A tour? I haven't worked there very long, Jake. I really don't think I'd be the best person to show her around. They have people in public relations who could do a better job."

"You know how it operates, you love your work, you love the kids. I don't think she could find anyone more qualified than you," he said.

"Why is she interested? She doesn't even live around here."

"No, she lives in Raleigh now," Jake answered.

"She's been offered a position at an institution similar to Smithfield in North Carolina. She's toured their facility, but she's having difficulty reaching a decision. When I told her about Smithfield, she thought seeing it might help her make up her mind."

Showing Karen Kingsley around Smithfield was not something Joanna had anticipated. It sounded potentially awkward. "I don't know."

But Jake continued, "She's not convinced she could be happy working in that setting. Maybe you could introduce her to some of the children and let her talk to one of the nurses."

"All right," Joanna agreed. "I won't be able to do it tomorrow, but my shift starts at three o'clock the next day. If she could be in the front office by two, I'll go in early to show her around."

"I'll give her a call in the morning to let her know," Jake answered. "Thank you."

"You're welcome."

"What hours are you working tomorrow?" he asked.

"The ten-hour shift I traded with Barb. From 9:30 p.m. to 7:30 a.m."

"Karen's husband is coming into town tomorrow, and we're going—"

Had she heard correctly? "Karen's husband?" Joanna repeated. "She's married?"

"Yes," he answered. "To Doug Kingsley."

"But I thought...I assumed... You didn't say she was married."

"You didn't ask," he replied. "We're going out

tomorrow night. Since you're free until nine-thirty, maybe you'd like to join us?''

"Jake, I couldn't," Joanna said suddenly, almost surprised to hear herself turning down the invitation. But Karen was a doctor...and her husband probably was, too. "I wouldn't know what to talk about."

"Talk about whatever you want to talk about...the same things you and I discuss."

"Three doctors and me? I don't think—''

"Two doctors, a minister and a social worker," Jake replied.

"A minister?" Joanna asked. "Karen's husband is a minister?"

"It surprised me, too," Jake commented with a grin. "The last time I spoke with him, he was a CPA." Jake stepped into the hallway. "Interested?"

"What time?" she asked.

"Seven o'clock."

"I'll be ready," she answered and closed the door as Jake walked down the hallway toward Mae's room. Glancing at the suitcase in the bottom of her closet, she knelt to push it back into its proper place. Then she opened the wooden jewelry box on the nightstand. Tucked safely beneath a few necklaces, she found the faded note kept from long ago. "Joanna, For your next move, which I hope is many years from now. Jake."

Had she loved him even then?

Joanna was ready early the next evening. Placing her jeans, T-shirt, socks and tennis shoes in her overnight bag, she was prepared to change her clothes as soon as she arrived at Smithfield later that night. The soft knit dress she had chosen to wear would not survive an hour of Freddie and companions.

Small gold hoop earrings perfectly accented the deep hunter-green outfit, and Joanna shook her head gently, allowing her ash-blond curls to softly frame her face. Lipstick, blush and a little mascara were applied, along with her favorite perfume.

Joanna studied her image in the mirror. "Well, this is as good as it's going to get," she sighed. She had never considered herself beautiful. Somewhat attractive would have been her self-appraisal, had she been forced to give one. She frowned at her reflection. Maybe if she'd been prettier. Older. Different. Oh, well. There was no sense in wondering about things she couldn't change. The Lord had made her the person she was. Joanna picked up her purse and the bag with her change of clothes in it and headed downstairs.

Ina was entering the front door with packages in her arms as Joanna descended the steps.

"Ina! Welcome home. How are the grandkids?"

"They're better. I'm the one who is exhausted." She looked over Joanna, from head to toe. "Where are you going? You look absolutely gorgeous."

"I'm going to dinner with Jake and the Kingsleys—friends of his."

"Do you always take an overnight bag with you when you leave for the evening?" Ina remarked, her voice raising in surprise.

"Only when I'm going to work afterward," Joanna replied. "I couldn't possibly work in this dress."

"So, you've been busy while I was away?"

"Yes," Joanna agreed.

"And Dr. Barnes? Everything is all right with him?"

"Everything's fine." Jake's voice startled them both and they looked toward the sound to see him entering the living room. "Glad you're back, Ina. Let me help you with those packages." He took the bundles from her arms, then caught sight of Joanna. And he didn't look away quickly. "Jo…"

Joanna couldn't help smiling. She apparently had achieved the look she was aiming for, if the admiration in Jake's eyes was any indication. "Hello, Jake."

The telephone rang loudly at the foot of the stairs, and Ina reached out to grab up the receiver.

"Dr. Barnes's residence. Yes?"

"We should go in separate cars tonight," Joanna suggested after it appeared that the call was not for either one of them. "I'll need to go directly to Smithfield from the restaurant." She continued down the steps to the hallway, not expecting a response.

"That's not necessary," he answered. "We're meeting Karen and Doug at the restaurant. You can take my car to work. They'll bring me home."

"Your car?" Joanna asked.

Just then, Ina's telephone conversation captured both Jake and Joanna's attention.

"Well, yes, Andrew. I'd love to," Ina said.

They both looked over at the mention of Andrew's name. Ina turned her back to them and continued talking, so Jake returned his attention to Joanna.

"Yes, you can take my car," he offered. "You'll

be home from work by eight o'clock in the morning, won't you? That's when I'll be leaving for the office.''

"Yes, but your car—" she protested.

"You can drive a five-speed. I taught you a couple of years ago."

"Yes, but it's expensive, Jake. I don't want to risk scratching it or—"

"Scratching it?" he repeated with a laugh. "What good is a car if you're afraid to drive it?"

"But I've already put one in a ditch since I've been here. The repairs on that must have cost a small fortune.''

"That was during a blizzard. That could happen to anyone," Jake argued.

Ina hung up the receiver.

"That was Andrew?" he asked.

"Yes," she replied with a grin and offered nothing more.

"Was it important?" he persisted.

"Very," Ina replied as she winked at Joanna before turning to walk away from the phone. "He asked me to go shopping with him."

"Shopping?" Jake repeated, but Joanna suddenly understood. In the past few weeks, she'd been so wrapped up in her own feelings, she had missed the obvious. Ina had feelings for someone, too. Andrew Vernon.

Without elaborating, Ina disappeared through the dining room, leaving Joanna on the steps, smiling and Jake standing nearby, frowning.

"Since when do Ina and Andrew shop together?" he asked. "I think I've missed something."

"I think we both have," Joanna agreed. "It looks like not all of Dr. Vernon's calls to this house are of a professional nature."

"I had no idea," Jake responded. "Andrew hasn't mentioned Ina to me."

Joanna's smile widened. "Looks like he'll be mentioning her now."

Chapter Nine

The restaurant was quaint, cozy and crowded when Jake and Joanna arrived that evening. Soon they were ushered to their reserved table in a dimly lit corner where Karen and Doug Kingsley were already seated.

Introductions were made, orders placed and Doug Kingsley offered a brief prayer of thanks. Joanna's choice of fantail shrimp had been seconded by Karen, but the baked potato, salad and homemade bread proved to be practically a meal within themselves.

The conversation flowed much more smoothly than Joanna had imagined. Doug Kingsley spoke freely of his conversion and call into the ministry, a discussion that was held primarily with Joanna since Karen and Jake had little to say on the subject.

Then dessert was refused by everyone except Karen, who had a small slice of cherry cheesecake and a large dose of teasing from the husband who obviously loved her very much. The evening had a way of slipping by much too quickly.

"Please excuse me," Joanna said after glancing reluctantly at her slender gold watch. "I'm afraid it's time for me to go to work."

"I'll be at Smithfield at two o'clock tomorrow," Karen reminded, "ready for the grand tour."

"I don't know how grand it will be, but I'll be there," Joanna replied with a smile before she and Jake excused themselves from the table. He escorted her out into the restaurant parking lot, his hand pressed lightly in the small of her back.

"Here are my keys," Jake said.

"I called a cab when Karen and I slipped away earlier to go to the ladies' room," Joanna explained. "But thank you for offering."

They retrieved Joanna's overnight bag from the back of Jake's automobile and were walking around the corner of the restaurant when they saw a cab rounding the curve and entering the lot.

"There was no need for this," Jake remarked.

"I know." She looked up into eyes sparking with irritation at her stubbornness. "But I feel better about going in a cab. I'm dependent upon you for too many things as it is."

Jake moved to speak to the cabdriver, but Joanna touched his arm, stopping him. "I'll take care of it. I have money," she assured him. "Now, go back inside and have a nice evening with your friends."

She released his arm and reached for the door, but Jake's hand covered hers, opening it for her. Joanna slid into the back seat.

"I wish you could stay," Jake admitted. "I've enjoyed the evening."

"Me, too," she replied, folding her hands together. "Very much."

"Call me when you're ready to come home in the morning, and I'll pick you up."

"Thank you. For tonight," she said.

He gave a slight nod. "Have I told you how beautiful you are?"

Her brown eyes flew open wide. No, he hadn't. And she was speechless.

"You are, Joanna. Too much so." Jake leaned into the cab, his mouth touching her temple in a light, lingering kiss. "See you in the morning," he added before closing the door.

"Ready, miss?" the driver asked.

"Yes," she said with a soft sigh. "I'm ready." Ready for more than Jake Barnes would probably ever choose to offer.

"Hey, Joanna!" It was Bob's voice coming across the Smithfield cafeteria in the early hours of morning.

"Bob's talkin' to you," Aaron and another child said simultaneously between bites of breakfast cereal.

"Thanks, guys, but I heard," she responded, taking a glass of orange juice from her own tray. "Good morning, Bob."

"I hear you need a ride home."

"I'm planning to call a cab," she answered. She had decided against disrupting Jake's morning with a call.

"No need. I'll drop you off on my way home," Bob offered. He set his tray down at the table where the children they were supervising were eating their breakfast.

"Does he like her?" Freddie asked rather loudly, inciting giggles from several of the kids nearby.

"No, Doc likes her," Aaron replied.

"Shh." Joanna frowned at the boys. "I live out in the country, Bob. It's probably out of your way."

"I don't mind. Seven-thirty?" he said.

"She likes Doc, too," Aaron's commentary continued.

"Aaron, please..."

But Bob persisted. "Can you be ready by then?"

"Definitely," she sighed. She had been ready to leave since the children had started an impromptu how-far-can-you-throw-your-banana-slices contest earlier that morning. Seven-thirty couldn't come soon enough.

"I warned you that it was out of your way," Joanna was saying a short time later as they traveled down a country road in Bob's older model pickup truck.

"No problem. Sure is pretty countryside out here."

"Yes, it is. Here's the house. The driveway is on the other side of those trees." She pointed toward the entrance, and he followed her directions.

"Some house," Bob commented while pulling up close to the sidewalk that led to the spacious front porch. Early daffodils and spring crocus were blooming everywhere and their array of colors accented the white paint of nearby fencing. "So, this is the doctor's home."

"Yes, it's Jake's. I'm just staying here until—"

"I know," Bob interrupted. "I heard the story from Barb."

He'd heard the story. Joanna wondered how many others had also. She opened the door to the truck to let herself out when Jake came out the front door with his jacket tossed over one shoulder and a briefcase in his hand. Joanna waved to him as she slid from the high truck seat.

Jake looked from Joanna, to the truck, to the driver. "I thought you were going to call."

"Bob offered to bring me home." Turning back toward the cab of the truck, she said, "This is Bob Youngston from Smithfield and Bob, this is Dr. Jake Barnes."

Jake barely acknowledged the young man's presence with only a slight nod of his head, then returned his piercing gaze to Joanna. "You should have called."

"But, there was no need. Bob didn't mind—"

"No, sir, I didn't," Bob agreed.

"Ina's holding breakfast for you," Jake stated sharply before walking away.

Joanna leaned back against the truck, watching as Jake started his car and left the driveway.

"Next time, maybe you'd better call, Joanna," Bob suggested. "He didn't seem too pleased with you."

"So I noticed," she remarked.

"I get the feeling I'm trespassing on private property."

"Of course, this is private property. It's Jake's home, but that doesn't mean you can't come on the grounds—"

"I'm not talking about real estate, Joanna. I mean you."

"Me?" she exclaimed. "Don't be silly. I'm not anyone's private property."

Bob studied her curiously. "Are you sure there's nothing going on between you and Dr. What's-his-name?"

"His name is Jake Barnes and, yes, I'm sure." She was almost sure. Wasn't she?

"I've gotta go," Bob said. "I'm working two until six this afternoon because someone called in sick. I've gotta get some sleep."

"I'm going in at two also." Joanna shut the truck door. "I'm giving a tour for an hour and then working until seven. Trading with Barb last night kind of messed up my schedule."

"Yep. Been there, done that." He grinned. "See you later."

"See you. Thanks again for the ride," she answered and headed toward the house. A brief hello to Mae and Ina, then a small breakfast preceded a few hours of sleep. Very few as it turned out.

"Hello, Karen." It was two o'clock exactly and Dr. Karen Kingsley was right on time. "Are you ready to see what Smithfield is all about?"

Joanna led the way through the front doors and into the dining area.

"How many children live here?" Karen's questions began.

"Ninety-five right now, but the number varies from week to week. Most children spend close to a year here before an appropriate placement is found. Then the child and adoptive parents or foster parents get acquainted before the child is discharged," Joanna explained as they walked through several different living areas, all decorated in cheerful colors.

"Are you involved in the counseling and the transitional process from resident to adoptive home?"

"No," Joanna responded. "I'm an aide for now. I supervise the children in the evenings and on weekends mostly. I'm going back to school in the fall to finish my degree."

"But the little boy you had with you at Jake's house? What's the purpose of your involvement with him?"

Joanna shrugged. "We like each other. I guess that's the main reason we spend time together. He came here after his last adoption failed, and he didn't have a regular volunteer to visit with, so I offered to be that person."

"Offered?" said the person who walked up behind them.

Joanna pivoted to come face-to-face with the assistant director. "Mrs. Southworth, I didn't realize you were here this afternoon."

"Giving a tour, are you?" The tone was light and friendly.

"Yes, I'd like you to meet Dr. Karen Kingsley,

and, Karen, this is Mrs. Frances Southworth, our assistant director here at Smithfield.''

"It's a pleasure to meet you." The greetings were brief, and Mrs. Southworth returned to her original comment. "I'd say that Joanna did more than offer to spend time with our little freckled-face Aaron. She persisted with her request until I finally gave in because I was too weary of the discussion to continue any longer." Mrs. Southworth continued to smile while Joanna's face flushed with color. "And I made a good decision in granting her extra time with the boy. I can see an improvement in his morale already."

"Thank you, Mrs. Southworth. Aaron does seem to be happy with the arrangement."

"Good, good," she responded. "Keep up the excellent work and please continue with the tour. It sounded as though you were doing a fine job. Thank you for stopping by, Dr. Kingsley."

"Mrs. Southworth, would you have a few free minutes to speak with Dr. Kingsley when I've finished showing her around?"

"Certainly. Stop in at the front office when you're finished. I'll be available until three-thirty." Then the assistant director left them alone to continue the tour.

"I don't know, Joanna. Nearly a hundred children, day in and day out. I don't think this would be for me. Seeing the same little faces all the time..." Karen was saying as they watched about twenty kids playing, or attempting to play, basketball.

Freddie scampered across the gym floor, chasing

the ball that had landed close to Karen's feet. "Hi, Jo-Jo!"

"Hello, Freddie. How's the game going?"

"Bad. I can't hit the basket!"

"Keep trying. Maybe Bob will help you," Joanna commented.

"He won't. He just keeps telling me to take turns and be nice and—"

"Maybe you should do those things. Then he wouldn't need to remind you so often." Joanna's suggestion brought a frown to the youngster's little round face, but it lasted only a moment.

"Guess what! We're gonna have play practice again tonight. Right after supper," he said.

"I saw that on the schedule," Joanna replied, wondering why the sudden burst of enthusiasm from Freddie over something he had grumbled about during the last few practices. "I didn't know you enjoyed it so much."

"I don't. Bein' a sunflower is stupid, but it's better than music lessons and as long as we keep practicing the play, we get to skip playin' the dumb piano."

"A real lover of the arts," Karen commented.

"Playing the piano won't hurt you, Freddie," Joanna insisted. "In fact, it's a very good thing to learn."

"It's dumb...it's for girls."

Joanna laughed softly. "It's for anyone who wants to learn."

"But I don't," he argued.

"Fred, get over here, please," Bob called from the other side of the gymnasium.

"You'll have to argue the piano lessons issue with Barbara. That's her decision," Joanna explained. "But the parts for the play were my decision, and I think you make a very handsome sunflower."

"No way, Jo-Jo—"

"Listen, Freddie," Joanna wanted to bring an end to a no-win conversation. "Bob wants you back over there with your other team members. You need to learn how to play nicely."

"What for? I still can't make a basket. Not ever!"

"How are you, Joanna?" The young man supervising the makeshift game waved across the court.

"Hi, Bob. Freddie needs some help shooting baskets."

"What Freddie needs is some help obeying the rules," was Bob's quick response. "C'mon, Fred. Let's try again."

"You're a pretty lady," Freddie said to Karen, ignoring Bob's words. "Wanna play ball with us?" He tried, unsuccessfully, to dribble the basketball as he spoke.

Bob was beside the child within seconds, stealing the ball from his hands. "Let's go, Fred. These ladies have better things to do than play basketball this afternoon."

"Bye, guys," Joanna said as they turned to exit the gym.

"Joanna." It was Bob's voice, and she glanced over her shoulder. "I need to talk to you before you leave tonight."

"About what?"

"Friday night," was the insufficient reply. "See me when you get a break."

"He seems like a nice young man," Karen stated. They stepped out into the hallway.

"Yes, Freddie is a challenge at times, but he—"

"No, I meant the supervisor. Bob? Was that his name?"

"Yes," Joanna answered. "Bob is very nice." Nice, helpful, good with the kids and interested in asking her something about Friday night apparently.

The tour concluded in the nurses' office, where Mrs. Southworth joined them for a question-and-answer period. Afterward, Joanna walked out to the parking lot with Karen.

"So? What do you think?"

"I think Smithfield is a wonderful place that helps displaced children put their lives back together," was Karen's response. "And I don't think I belong in this type of setting, no matter how important the work that is done here proves to be."

"But why?" Joanna asked. "If you think this is such a good place—"

"Is playing basketball something you do with the kids?" Karen opened her car door as she spoke.

A frown curved Joanna's mouth. "Yes, but it's part of my job."

"But you'd do it, anyway. Wouldn't you? Basketball, baseball, whatever…whether it was part of your job or not."

"Yes, but—" Joanna began.

"I wouldn't," Karen answered flatly. "I see children four and a half days a week in my office, and I do the best I can for them, Joanna. Really I do. But working with them, relating to them in a setting so similar to home—"

"This is their home, Karen. Temporarily, at least. They have to feel as though it is," Joanna defended.

"I realize that fact, and I should have realized it when I toured the children's home that offered me the job."

"But you're a doctor, Karen. You wouldn't be expected to play with the children or to supervise them. Jake comes here every Wednesday to treat the kids' illnesses and injuries. He doesn't play basketball with them."

Karen smiled and squeezed Joanna's hand. "They need a physician who can give more of herself than I can. It would be a job to me. That's all. I don't have children of my own, and I could never give as much affection to the residents as I should...as they need."

"You never know. You might have more of yourself to give than you think. Maybe you'd even meet a child you'd want to adopt—"

"No," came the blunt response. "That's not what I want. Working around needy children all day, every day..." Karen climbed into her car and pulled down the visor, blocking the glare of the sun. "It wouldn't benefit the children enough to justify it, and it would be too painful for me."

Painful... Joanna didn't understand but asking didn't seem appropriate. She waited for Karen to continue.

"Thank you, Joanna, for your time and your friendliness. We need institutions like Smithfield, and I hope you continue your work here for many years.''

Joanna raised a hand, shading her own eyes from the sunlight. "I won't be here much longer, Karen.''

"You're not really thinking of leaving, are you? Jake mentioned that you'd be moving out as soon as Mae felt she could return home. Surely you won't leave that little boy you've spent so much time with.''

"I'll have to go when the time comes. I have another year of school to complete in South Carolina. That's my home.''

"I would think your supervisor here would hate to see you go...as will Aaron and Jake.''

A bittersweet smile curved Joanna's lips. "Thanks, but Smithfield, Aaron and Jake all got along fine before I arrived. I'm sure they'll go on quite well without me.''

"I'm not so certain about that," Karen began, "but if you do go south again, stop in Raleigh and we'll have lunch. I'll even show you the children's home that I won't be working in.'' She smiled.

"Maybe I'll do that," Joanna replied as Karen started her car. "Take care.''

"You, too. Thanks for everything and, Joanna, if I were you, I'd tell Bob I was busy on Friday. Then I'd ask Jake if he's free.''

"You have a vivid imagination," Joanna answered. "Bob probably wants to switch schedules with me, and Jake—'' She stopped.

"And Jake?" Karen repeated. "You're interested, aren't you?''

"Yes, but—''

"The Lord helps those who help themselves, Joanna." Karen's light laugh floated through the air. "Of course, Doug keeps telling me that's not in the Bible."

"If it is, I haven't found it yet," Joanna responded with a pleasant smile. "But thanks for the advice."

"Doug wanted me to be sure to tell you that after you left last night, he and Jake got into quite a lengthy discussion about prayer."

"They did? Was it interesting?"

Karen thought for a few seconds before responding. "Those discussions are always interesting, but Jake seemed more into it than I was. Doug and I have talked endless hours about his conversion and decision to enter the ministry. I keep telling him someday I'll come around to his way of thinking. Not yet. Not now. But Jake...I don't know. He had such specific questions."

"That's good," Joanna replied, straining to conceal the emotion that threatened to crack her voice. "Maybe he's been thinking about God. Everyone needs to."

"So I've been told," Karen responded, the smile returning to her fair face. "Listen, I've got to run, but Doug wanted you to know about the discussion. He seemed to think it would mean a lot to you."

"Thank you. Have a safe trip home," she called to Karen as she watched her drive away.

Doug had been right. The information did mean a lot to her aching heart. Jake needed the Lord in his life, and maybe a "not yet" answer was nearing the "yes" stage. She hurried back into the building to make her three o'clock shift on time.

And Bob's question did pertain to scheduling—but not work hours. He invited her to go out for dinner after their shift on the following Friday evening.

"How was shopping yesterday?" Joanna asked when she had a moment alone with Ina the next morning. "Did you and Andrew have a good time?" Ina had just returned from an early trip to the supermarket and was in the kitchen unloading sacks of groceries.

"Marvelous," Ina replied as she put several boxes into the cupboard. "You and Dr. Barnes should try it sometime."

"Shopping?" Joanna picked up several bags of frozen vegetables and placed them in the freezer.

"It could lead to better things," Ina remarked.

"Then maybe we should," Joanna agreed with a shrug before sliding a box of pancake batter into the cupboard over the sink.

"Andrew and I went to the mall last night to buy a jacket for his son's birthday." Ina folded an empty grocery bag. "I guess we're living proof that romance doesn't have to end at any age."

Joanna smiled. "I already know that, Ina, but I was a little slow in picking up on your interest in Andrew."

"So was he," Ina complained. "He's been nice and polite for months, but he's finally noticing. We only went shopping for a few hours, but it's a beginning."

"Yes, it is," Joanna agreed. But sometimes beginnings didn't lead anywhere. She wished for happier endings for Ina and Andrew than she had experienced. "Where's Jake?"

"I think he went for a walk." Ina looked toward the back door, and then toward Joanna. "Would you see if I left my keys in the car?"

"Sure. Why did you do the grocery shopping so early this morning? You must have left the house at the crack of dawn."

"If you wait until the last minute, sometimes all of the sale items are gone."

"The last minute? Ina, it's not even eight o'clock yet."

"Maybe not, but Andrew has breakfast at the in-store restaurant every morning," Ina confessed. "So I did the grocery shopping early enough that I could run into him there. Would you check for my keys, please?"

"Okay." But before Joanna even disappeared through the door, she added, "You're not going to buy this many groceries every time you want to see Andrew, are you? I don't think we can eat this much."

"Go on," Ina shooed her away and then reached toward the counter. Picking up the keys in question, she slipped them into her pocket with a grin.

Joanna walked toward Ina's station wagon, cutting through a backyard filled with signs of spring. Purple crocus and yellow daffodils lined the driveway she was approaching.

"Good morning."

She turned in the direction of the voice. "Jake?"

"Over here." He was leaning against the fence railing on the other side of the garage, overlooking the fields and nearby woods.

She walked toward him. The morning was a beautiful one, too lovely to disturb with needless words. Joining him on the railing, she slipped her foot onto the first rung, stepped up, raising herself up to nearly his height. Together they stood viewing the landscape as Joanna thought of yesterday.

"Jake, I'm sorry I didn't call you yesterday for a ride home. It's just that I hate being a bother to you."

"You're never a bother, Jo," he answered, then paused. "I guess I should apologize for not being friendly to your young driver." He glanced at her before returning his gaze to the horizon. "He made me remember being twenty-two. I didn't care much for the feeling."

"Why not?" Joanna asked.

"I don't know," he said. "Maybe just because it was so long ago." He was silent for a moment before he continued, "I used to come out here every morning when I was a boy." Then offered nothing more.

But Joanna didn't mind the lack of conversation. She did not need more than to know this was a special place, and that he was willing to share it with her. The trees in the woods were beginning to bud, and all traces of winter had vanished.

"It's lovely, Jake," she said softly, and then reached to retie the slender black ribbon that was slipping from her hair.

He turned toward her, studying her delicate profile in the early morning sunlight. But when Joanna tilted her head to search his warm gray eyes, he looked away and returned his gaze to the woods.

"This is the first time I've stood here since last fall."

"That's a shame," she said. "It's such a peaceful place."

"When I first moved back into this old house, I'd walk out here occasionally before leaving for the office."

Joanna listened. Why had he quit coming here? Why was he here this morning? Why today and why with her?

"When I was a kid, I used to sit on that fence post and think about what I wanted to do with my life."

Joanna's heartbeat quickened. "Is that why you're here today?"

Jake glanced at her again before looking down at the white railing. "I don't know. Maybe."

Maybe; maybe not. Joanna pushed a few strands of hair from her temple and waited.

"I decided to go to medical school...planned it all sitting right here." He placed the palm of his hand against the wood. "Of course, things didn't go exactly as the twelve-year-old imagined, but fairly close."

"The clinic? And taking over your father's practice? Were those things in your plans?"

"No, but some of the changes were for the better."

And some for the worse, Joanna considered. "And now?"

"I don't know," he replied. "I'm not sure any more."

"You're a doctor, Jake," she spoke in a soft voice. "People pay you to be sure."

"For them, I'm sure. As much as I can be, anyway. But for myself...that's a different story."

A slight breeze, refreshingly cool, rustled the branches overhead. Jake turned, looking out toward the driveway. "I think fence post decision making works better for twelve-year-olds than someone in his midthirties."

"Maybe so," she responded with a sweet smile as she stepped down from the railing.

Jake extended a hand to her. "C'mon. I've got to get going."

Joanna reached out, letting him clasp her hand securely in his, and they walked toward the back door.

They had no more than entered the kitchen, when Ina greeted them with a message. "Dr. Barnes, you had a call from a Dr. Eden while you were outside. She said she'd call back later."

"All right. Thank you, Ina," Jake replied and picked up his jacket and tie. "See you tonight." And he was on his way to the office.

"We were only out at the back fence, Ina. You could have let him know that Dr. Eden was on the phone," Joanna said, helping Ina put away the remaining canned goods.

"You and Dr. Barnes rarely have a moment alone together." Ina shut the cupboard door loudly. "Dr. Eden can call him later. A second long distance call won't hurt her a bit. In fact, maybe it will discourage her a little."

"I doubt that. Oh, I forgot your keys," Joanna suddenly remembered. "I'll run out to get them."

"No need." Ina patted the pocket of her sweater. "I found them on the counter."

"Before or after you sent me outside to look for them?" Joanna asked, eyeing her friend suspiciously.

"You ask too many questions, dear."

Too many with Ina, not enough with Jake? Joanna wasn't certain about that, and she had no idea that the questions she had answered for someone else only a short time ago, would lead to such a pleasant surprise later that morning. Mrs. Southworth was the bearer of good news upon Joanna's arrival at Smithfield.

"Is Jake here?" Joanna was nearly breathless later in the day as she spoke to the receptionist at Jake's office through the glass partition. "Has he left for lunch yet?"

"No, Miss Meccord. He's on the telephone."

"I need to see him as soon as he's finished. It will only take a minute."

"I'll tell him you're here. Please, wait just a moment." The receptionist answered and turned away from the window.

"Jake!" Joanna exclaimed when she saw him walk into the area, not far from the front desk.

He looked up from the prescription he was writing, but Joanna had left the window to open the door leading from the waiting room into the office.

"Oh, Jake, you won't believe what happened! You won't believe it!" she cried as she rounded the corner, coming face-to-face with him. She placed both hands on his arm while the secretary and receptionist looked on with interest.

"What won't I believe?" he asked, placing the pad and pen on the nearby desk. The slightest hint of a lazy smile played at one corner of his mouth.

"You already know, don't you?" she accused. "I thought you'd be surprised—"

"Surprises?" Andrew had entered the room so quietly, no one had noticed his arrival.

She turned, without releasing her grip on Jake's arm, to greet his partner. "Hi, Andrew. How are you?"

"I'm fine, but what's this surprise you were referring to? Aren't you going to share it with us?"

"I guess I could," she said with a shrug. "It's—"

"Wait a minute," Jake interrupted. "I want to hear this privately first," he added, smiling. "Let's go into my office."

So down the narrow hallway they went into a comfortable, darkly paneled room.

"She told you, didn't she? Before I even knew!" Joanna exclaimed with a pretense of a frown turning her mouth down.

"Who?" he asked as he reached out to catch her hand in his.

"Karen Kingsley," Joanna answered, squeezing the fingers that touched hers. "She donated twenty thousand dollars to Smithfield. Twenty thousand dollars, Jake! And all because of the children she met and the things Mrs. Southworth told her and the report of the annual budget and—'' She had to stop when she ran out of breath.

''It's a good thing you agreed to give her that tour,'' he commented, smiling broadly.

''Did you know? Did she tell you she was thinking of making the contribution?''

He shook his head. ''I had no idea until Doug called this morning. Karen is unpredictable.''

''Unpredictable, maybe, but wonderful! Generous! And rich! She must be to give away money like that.''

''She comes from a wealthy family. Old money. She can afford it,'' he replied, running his thumb across the back of Joanna's hand.

''But I thought she wasn't impressed. I mean, she decided against taking the job she'd been considering after less than an hour at Smithfield.''

''Doug said she realized she could never work so closely with the same children, day after day. It would be too difficult for her knowing she can't have a baby of her own.''

''But, Jake...I didn't realize...''

''I didn't, either, until Doug explained it this morning. They just found out a few weeks ago, and Karen isn't ready to talk about it,'' he said. ''She was really impressed with the work there, Jo, but she was upset by how worn most of the furniture looked. She wanted to make some contribution toward improvement.''

''And she certainly did! Mrs. Southworth told me that the remodeling will begin in about a month.''

''That's great. Karen and Doug will be pleased.''

''But I feel almost guilty about it, Jake. When I

first met Karen, I didn't think I was going to like her. Then, after I got to know her better, she was so friendly to me, and now to learn how generous she's been—''

"That will teach you not to judge people at first glance." Jake paused, looking down at the hand he held so seldom. "Go to lunch with me?"

"I'd love to, but—" she looked down at her jeans and oversize yellow shirt "—I'm not dressed for it. I was at work this morning helping the kids with arts and crafts, and I'm a mess."

"You look fine," he assured her, releasing her hand and removing his white coat.

"But your patients—" she protested.

"No more until two o'clock," he countered. "Let's go."

"But I look awful, and you..." She took a quick survey. "Your clothes, that tie—you look too good."

"Think so, huh?" he teased. "If it will make you happier, I won't put on the sports coat. And this tie—" he unknotted the tie and slid it free from his shirt "—can come off." He touched her hand again, recapturing it. "C'mon, I'm hungry."

And she was ushered down the hallway, despite her minor protests.

"The news was worth celebrating, I take it?" Andrew asked as they walked past him.

"Definitely. I'll tell you all about it when I get back," Jake replied before informing the receptionist what time he would return. Then they headed out the side door to find a good place to have lunch.

"I'll have ham and cheese with lettuce. Yes, mustard, please," she was telling the woman at the deli. And there were pretzels and pickles...and a large glazed doughnut for dessert.

They sat down at a tiny round table for two at the far side of the crowded restaurant. Joanna bowed her head and offered a silent prayer. Jake waited, as he'd grown accustomed to doing. Then they ate their meal together.

Jake finished his sandwich first and was eating some of Joanna's pretzels while she talked about the remodeling plans for Smithfield.

"How can you eat all of that and stay so thin?" he asked after watching her bite into the sugar-coated dessert.

"It's the shirt." She tugged on the tail of her roomy top. "It makes me look skinny. Want a bite?" she asked and with a smile she held the pastry up for his inspection.

Jake shook his head, laughing. "It's all yours."

"This is one of the best doughnuts I've ever eaten," she said. Maybe it wasn't the pastry; maybe it was the company. "You don't know what you're missing."

"Yes," Jake responded, his voice suddenly low and remote. "I think I do."

She placed the doughnut on her saucer and wiped her fingers with a paper napkin. If Jake was missing someone, it couldn't be her, she reasoned, since she was seated right there in front of him. And Dr. Natalie Eden was the only woman she could think of who might still be breaking his heart. The dessert no longer seemed tempting as the silence surrounded them in the midst of the noisy deli crowd.

She looked up to see him staring out the nearby window. She'd felt alone most of her life, but she'd never known anything lonelier than this—loving a man who couldn't love her back.

"I'm supposed to be at work soon." She made a feeble, but honest excuse. "I'd better be going."

"I'll walk with you—"

"No, please," she replied, standing up as Jake's concerned gaze met her watery brown eyes. "I'll go alone. Thank you for lunch," she said and with those words, she slipped away from him, making her way through the congested restaurant to the busy downtown sidewalk.

Jake watched her walk until the bright shirt she wore was little more than a yellow blur blocks away. He placed a hand wearily against his forehead, remembering the hurt he had seen in her eyes, today and how many yesterdays? How much longer could they hover this close to a love they both wanted but couldn't have? He was more acutely aware than ever of the life he was missing. Time spent with Joanna only reminded him of all they didn't share. They couldn't remain simply friends, they couldn't be lovers. And he had no stomach for the idea of repeating his father's mistakes. Marrying a sweet young thing who would grow up and move on some day.

Jake pushed away from the table, stood and strode toward the door. Anger coursed through him as he stepped out into the midday sunshine. But his conscience wouldn't allow him to continue on in that vein of thought. Joanna couldn't be considered a "sweet young thing." Not by anyone. No, she was far more than that, more than he wanted her to be. She didn't fit into any category, and she was driving him mad with trying to put her into one. One he could live with. Or without.

Chapter Ten

"Natalie Eden is coming for the weekend," Jake said as he stood by the dining room table with an open file folder in his hands.

Joanna was startled, although she knew she shouldn't be. Natalie Eden was the answer to questions Jake hadn't asked. Like with whom should he spend the rest of his life.

"I'm sure you'll be glad to see each other," she somehow said in an even voice. "It's been quite a while, hasn't it?"

Without looking up from the report he was reading, Jake responded, "She's coming to see the new wing of the hospital."

But Dr. Eden had called Jake to let him know she was coming, hadn't she? That's probably the call Ina had mentioned the other day when Jake and Joanna had been talking out by the back fence. Joanna had let the hope take root that maybe he'd been thinking about a future with her that day. Or maybe he'd been contemplating letting the Lord into his heart. But more than likely, Natalie had been the one on his mind, even then. And Dr. Eden probably had little, if any, interest in a wing of any hospital. She'd be coming to see Jake. To remind, renew, rekindle.

Joanna gathered up her library books from the table, stacking them noisily together.

Jake glanced up from the paperwork and watched Joanna's abrupt movements.

"It's nothing personal, Joanna," he remarked, closing the folder he held in his hand and sliding it into his briefcase. "I'm meeting her at the airport late Friday evening, and we're going to get something to eat. That's all."

"She's coming to visit a hospital, but she's having dinner with you," Joanna commented. "How convenient."

"Natalie is someone I went to school with," he answered, looking into her stormy eyes. "I'm taking her out to eat and then dropping her at the hotel next to the hospital. Nothing more."

Nothing more. Sure, she wanted to say. Joanna blinked back hot tears, jealous of things she wasn't even certain had happened. How could she feel this way? Natalie Eden would probably believe her to be jealous. Possessive. Resentful of Natalie's presence in Jake's world. She would be accurate in her thinking no matter how much Joanna wished she wasn't.

"I hope you have a good time," Joanna said rather nicely, considering the way she felt inside. "I have a date that night, too." The childish words surprised even her. Joanna could hardly believe she'd spoken them.

Jake regarded her quizzically for a moment. "A date? With whom?"

"With Bob from work." Joanna's face flushed, but she continued with the fabrication. She was in too deep to bail out now. She couldn't stand the thought of seeing Jake and Natalie together again. Enjoying each other's company. One thing would lead to another.... And Bob *had* asked her to go out with him this Friday night. She had politely refused at the time, but maybe it wasn't too late to reconsider.

"Bob," he repeated the name. "The guy that brought you home that morning? When did you start seeing him?"

"What difference does it make?" Joanna responded, realizing that one untrue statement in this conversation was plenty. "It looks like we'll both be busy on Friday evening."

Jake stood silently studying her face for a moment. He wondered if she knew how little it took to arouse old fears and uncertainties in him that he'd long tried to put to rest.

"I've got to be going, or I'll be late for work," Joanna said and started toward the door away from his scrutiny. "See you later."

She wasn't sure whether or not Jake responded, and she didn't really care. All she wanted was to escape, to go to work...anywhere that would keep her mind busy. Natalie Eden was coming back into Jake's life. Just for the weekend. But a weekend was time enough to accomplish what she'd come for. Joanna didn't even want to think about it.

Trying to come up with a way to see if Bob's invitation for Friday evening was still open was suddenly made easy. The young man with blond hair and eyes that were a friendly brown approached her in the dining hall at Smithfield during lunch. He casually asked her to pass the ketchup and mentioned that Friday night was still a possibility, if she was interested. And interested she was.

Friday night brought a steak dinner and a movie. Unfortunately for Joanna, the latest romantic film to be released was Bob's suggestion. She couldn't seem to sway him in another direction, not for lack of trying.

Spending a few hours with Bob outside of Smithfield was pleasant enough. His only noticeable flaw was one he couldn't do anything about. He wasn't Jake Barnes. And Jake was the man she was in love with. Pure and simple. Now and maybe forever. But she couldn't tell anyone else that. No one but the Lord, and she wasn't convinced He was listening much these days. She glanced skyward at the thought.

Bob eventually took her to her car in the Smithfield parking lot. He didn't try to kiss her, and Joanna was relieved. She had no intention of kissing him and she hadn't yet thought of a polite way to avoid it. He simply reached for her hand. "You know, you should rethink that relationship of yours with the doctor."

Joanna frowned a little. "What do you mean?"

"I mean, whether you know it or not, you're crazy

about someone and my guess is it's the disgruntled Dr. Barnes.'' Bob smiled and shook his head. ''I don't know what you'd see in him though, honestly, Joanna. He's only tall, rich and handsome.''

''Bob—''

''Don't try to tell me I'm wrong.'' Bob squeezed her hand before letting go. ''He was ready to take my head off that day I gave you a ride home from work. Whatever was going on between the two of you that morning had a lot to do with something other than your choice of transportation for the day.''

''I'm sorry, Bob. I shouldn't have agreed to go out with you under the circumstances. I guess that's why I insisted on paying for my own dinner and movie ticket.''

''I figured that had something to do with it,'' Bob admitted. ''That and your protest about seeing a romantic movie. I knew there had to be a reason for it, and a broken heart was a good guess.''

''I'm sorry,'' she said. Then they stood in awkward silence for a moment before she added. ''I don't want to feel this way about him, but it's something I can't seem to get away from.''

''Have you known him for a long time?''

''Four years,'' Joanna answered.

''Four years,'' Bob said thoughtfully and looked out toward the busy highway. ''Too bad. I thought maybe this was something new with you. You know, the I met him and fell for him before I really knew him kind of thing.''

''No, that's not it,'' Joanna said with a slight shake of her head. ''It's much more.''

Bob shrugged his shoulders. "Then go for it. If you haven't told him how you feel, do it. What's the worst that can happen? You find out he doesn't feel the same about you? You're already living with that pain. You may as well find out if it's for real or not." He grinned. "And if he's not interested, tell him he's not smart enough to be a doctor. Then call me. We'll try again. Next time, I'm buying."

Joanna leaned forward and gave him a quick peck on the cheek. "Thank you. You're good for my ego," she admitted. Then she got into her car, and Bob shut the door for her.

"Good night, Joanna. See you tomorrow," he said before she drove away from Smithfield toward home. Jake's home.

Glancing at her watch, she saw it was nearly midnight and wondered if he'd be there. Or if he was still with Natalie Eden. Joanna didn't like the possibilities.

Chapter Eleven

Shortly after midnight, Joanna pulled into the driveway. Jake's car was parked near the garage where it usually was this time of night, and relief came over her at the sight. If it hadn't been there, she probably would have sat down on the front steps and wept from sheer jealousy.

Joanna got out of her car and headed toward the house, grateful for the porch light Ina had left burning. But she was in no hurry as she approached the front door. She wasn't tired. Just discouraged. Sad. Lonely. Turning the key in the lock, she slipped quietly into the sleeping house. The door clicked shut behind her as she switched off the outside light and turned to find the hand railing of the staircase. Then she made her way up the steps in the darkness. Walking into her bedroom, she dropped her purse on the dresser and kicked off her shoes. When Joanna pulled back the bedspread, the sheets felt cool beneath her fingertips. She folded them down. Maybe she was a little bit tired, after all, she considered. And definitely thirsty. The popcorn at the theater had been too salty for her taste. Her mind went back to the events of the evening.

Her date with Bob had not lasted long, but she'd missed Jake the whole time. Every single minute. She picked up her pillow and gave it a halfhearted punch. Was she forever the hopeless romantic who would want someone she couldn't have? Sometimes it felt that way deep inside, and she wanted to kick herself for allowing it to happen.

With a frustrated groan, she headed for the bathroom to get a drink. The tap water from the sink wasn't very cold, and she remembered the pitcher of water Ina kept in the refrigerator. Still wearing her jeans and pink T-shirt from work, Joanna descended the staircase quickly, her bare feet sinking into the plush carpeting. She walked through the darkness into the kitchen. As she pulled open the refrigerator door, the cool air flowed over her. The light from within dispelled the shadows of the room, and Joanna gasped when she saw a movement near the table.

"It's just me." Jake's voice cut through the night.

She closed the appliance door abruptly. "Why are you sitting here in the dark?"

"Can't sleep when I'm angry," he stated flatly.

Joanna watched him lift a glass to his mouth and take a long, slow drink as she walked toward the table. Her mind went back to his story of little Toby's death in the emergency room. And the drinking that followed. "You're angry with me?" she asked cautiously.

Jake gave no reply. His glare remained on her eyes until it lowered to her lips, which were still parted in question.

Joanna's heart thumped uncomfortably as unwelcome tension stretched between them. But the conclusion she'd reached earlier that evening preyed upon her conscience.

"Jake, driving home tonight I thought of the way I acted about your date with Natalie Eden—"

"It wasn't a date."

He was going to make this difficult for her, and she knew she deserved it. She placed her unsteady hands on the back of the chair in front of her, gripping it firmly.

"Well, whatever it was," she began, "I was wrong to act the way I did about it. You have the freedom to see whomever you wish." Even if it shatters my heart into tiny bits, she longed to say. Nervously, she ran her thumb along the back of the wooden chair in front of her and waited for a response. For his forgiveness. She'd never dreamed he wouldn't give it.

"Is that why you came down here in the middle of the night? To apologize to me?" One eyebrow quirked in sarcastic inquiry. The moon filtered enough light through the window to ease the darkness of the room and reveal the bitterness in the direct gaze that viewed her.

"No, I—" Why had she come down here? "I didn't realize you were here. I came to get a drink."

"Have one." He pushed his glass across the table

toward her. "Then go back to bed," he ordered and looked away as something dangerously close to despair stole over his features.

His demand came harshly, but the sharp response that came so easily to the tip of Joanna's tongue was silenced by the anguish she'd glimpsed in his gaze. "Jake—"

"So, tell me," he interrupted, his eyes meeting hers again. The sorrow was gone, replaced by anger. Or was it something else? "What did you and that date of yours do tonight?" His low, almost threatening words startled her.

"I don't like what you're implying," she answered over the uneasy thudding in her chest. "We went out to get something to eat after work and saw a movie together. That's all." Wanting to put some distance between them, she returned to the refrigerator and poured water into a glass.

"That had better be all." Jake's tone was sharp, the meaning clear. "This is the first time in my life I've ever waited for someone to come home from a date. I didn't know whether to feel like a worried guardian or just plain jealous."

"The fact is, you're neither." Joanna took a sip of water as she watched him, her misgivings increasing. What did he want from her? Why was she continually receiving these mixed signals from him? "Why did you wait for me, Jake? You could be with Natalie. Isn't that where you'd rather be?" She placed the glass on the counter abruptly, spilling some of the contents.

"No, it isn't," he snapped. "Natalie Eden is here to see the hospital."

"She couldn't care less about any hospital." Joanna almost choked on the words. "It's you she's after, Jake, and you know it." Her eyes filled with tears suddenly, unexpectedly. The sob rising in her throat nearly cut off her words, and she raised an arm, covering her mouth with the back of her hand.

Jake rose from his chair and moved toward her. "It's not like that."

Joanna wiped away angry tears. "Yes, it is. She wants you—"

"Jo, don't—"

"—and you're always here for her...waiting."

Jake's hands brushed her arms, gliding up to her shoulders. "Natalie is not who I'm waiting for."

Joanna swallowed hard. She could barely comprehend what she'd heard until his warm, unsteady hands touched her face.

His fingers moved to sift through the softness of her hair, and Jake wondered how he'd kept from kissing her the thousand different times he'd wanted to. He'd never felt this way with any woman. None except this one. "You are who I want, who I've always wanted, Joanna."

She gasped in pure amazement. She'd nearly given up hope that he'd ever say such things to her. Her throat ached with words she longed to say in return but wouldn't. Not until she knew his heart and the secrets kept there. What Joanna didn't realize was that her eyes told Jake what he needed to know. The love they'd not spoken of was mutual. Deep. He saw it shining in her hopeful gaze as his hands found her waist, pulling her close. She was the most precious thing in his life. The only thing that mattered. He wanted to never let her go.

Jake slowly lowered his mouth, capturing hers in a kiss he meant to be gentle. But Joanna responded with yearning she was too young and trusting to hide. She was soft and beautiful, warm and giving, and Jake's hands moved against the soft lines of her back, arching her toward him. Joanna was everything he'd longed for, right there in his arms. Together they were discovering a love they hadn't been aware they could feel until they found each other.

"Jake," she murmured his name as his mouth left her soft lips for the slender column of her throat.

Raising his head, he looked into those beautiful eyes so filled with unspoken emotion.

They'd been here before—that night of Joanna's birthday, the snowy evening by the firelight, a hundred times or more in their dreams.

Jake looked away for a moment to fight an unfamiliar sting in his own eyes. This ache in his heart went way beyond wanting. It had for a long time. He loved her. No matter how much he didn't want to, he did. It was deep and real. And it hurt like nothing he'd ever imagined.

He pulled her close, breathing warm words against her temple. "What am I going to do with you, Jo? You're here, around all the edges of my life, without really being mine at all. And I know I can't have you, but I don't want to let you go."

"Does it have to be all or nothing?" she asked in

a sad whisper as she tipped her head up to meet his gaze.

"Either one will break our hearts," he said quietly. Jake leaned forward to kiss her lightly on the mouth before releasing her.

It felt like a kiss goodbye. Panic rose in her throat. "Jake—"

"Go back upstairs, Joanna. You don't belong down here with me."

"But I don't want to leave you." He was slipping away, shutting her out, and she reached for his arm, wanting desperately to hold on to the best of what they'd found in each other's hearts. "We can't keep doing this to ourselves...to each other."

But Jake's hand encircled her wrist, removing her hand from his arm and pressing it down to her side. He had to force himself to meet her gaze, not wanting to confront the misery he knew he'd find there. The same misery she'd seen in him.

"We have something special, Jake. Far more than friendship. We both feel it every time we touch."

"Yes, we do," he agreed. "That's why I can't be your friend," he sighed in self-disgust. "I can't keep my hands off you long enough for that. And we can't be lovers. That would go against everything you believe in." Jake paused, studying her sorrowful expression. There was marriage, of course. Being a husband, having a wife. He'd steered clear of it all his life. But, now, with Joanna....

Tell him...tell him. Ina's words ran through Joanna's mind once again. Her love for Jake burned brighter than ever, but could she risk telling him when he had not spoken of love? She lowered her gaze to the collar of his shirt.

"Jake, what we have...this can't be only physical. Please tell me you want more than that." Her voice was soft and pleading, and her heart was afraid of his reply.

"Of course, it's more," he responded, openly surprised by the honesty in her statement. "How can you ask that? Look at me, Jo."

She hesitantly met his solemn gaze again, and in that instant he wanted to tell her everything. How much he loved her, how much he wanted a lifetime with her. But she couldn't promise him forever. Could she? At her age? "You know it's much more."

Joanna stood only inches from him but the distance seemed intolerable, and she moved easily into the embrace that was there for the taking. "Oh, Jake..."

Jake's arms went around her in a protective band of warmth, his mouth barely brushing her forehead. "You belong with someone your own age, someone who shares your beliefs and convictions." But the thought of Joanna finding that someone had never come so close as tonight when she'd been out with Bob. The threat of it seemed to twist and turn inside Jake. The affection she'd so freely offered was a treasure he'd rejected. Time and again. And tonight, sitting alone in that dark kitchen, how he'd wished she'd come home. Watching her fall in love with another man was something he wouldn't do. He couldn't. Jake cupped her face tenderly in his hands again and looked into those dark, dark eyes in which he sometimes felt he could almost drown. And he knew deep down for the first time that he'd rather drown there than lose her. "God forgive me, I can't let you go," he whispered the truth his heart finally accepted.

Joanna's eyes flew open wide. "Do you mean that?"

"Yes," he admitted. "I want you. Us." His hands were warm against her face, framing it, caressing it. "I don't know how I've fought it this long." He smiled a little before his mouth met hers again with a sweet tenderness that easily brought tears to Joanna's eyes.

She was all he loved in this life. If what they shared didn't last forever, he'd take whatever they could have. He'd settle for that. He had to. If he lost her someday and was destined to live his father's sorrow over again, then he'd have to find a way to survive it. He couldn't let her go now.

Joanna responded to his kiss with all the hope in her young heart until Jake slowly brought the moment to an end and pressed his lips in a last, light touch on the tip of her nose. He wasn't sure if he'd lost this battle, or won it. Joanna made him believe in possibilities he hadn't dare think of before falling in love. Things like promises, commitment, the future. With her. Things he would offer. Things he would ask. "Joanna...I want to do this right."

Then it was Joanna's turn to smile. She had ideas. Possibilities of her own. "I know how we can start. Remember when we went to dinner with Karen and Doug? And the night we celebrated my birthday? I loved those times together, and we've done so few things like that, Jake. Couldn't we try? Just the two of us?'' She paused, catching her lower lip anxiously between her teeth as she waited for his reaction.

"Something not too tempting?" he remarked, his steady gaze arousing that familiar longing in Joanna, a longing Jake easily recognized.

She watched him glance away from her momentarily as if considering something, and when he looked fully at her again, a glint of amusement brightened his expression. "Are you asking me for a date?"

"Not if you're going to laugh, no," she countered briskly and dropped her gaze to the floor.

"I'm not laughing." With one warm hand he touched her chin, gently tilting it up until his own eyes once again locked with wary brown. "It's just a little out of character for you, that's all."

"I have a bad habit of doing things out of character when you're involved."

One corner of Jake's mouth curved into a smile. "Believe me, Joanna, I've noticed. And, yes, we'll go somewhere tomorrow evening. Any place you choose is fine. Except here, alone in this house, in the dark." His smile faded. "Understood?"

She laughed softly although she hardly felt like laughing at all. "Understood," she responded and reached up to slide her fingers into his silky straight hair.

But Jake caught her wrist gently and brought it to his mouth for a whispery kiss. Joanna stood perfectly still, entranced by the teasing touch of his lips against her skin.

Jake cleared his throat, pretending not to be affected by the glimpse of pure desire Joanna had unknowingly given. He let go of her arm slowly. This wasn't going to be easy. "I want to do this the right way, Jo. Your way."

She nodded, unable to speak with her breath in her throat the way it was.

"Go upstairs. Now." He inclined his head toward the kitchen doorway and let her hand slip from him. "Before I try to talk you into staying."

"But, Jake—"

Firm hands moved to her shoulders. "Please, Joanna. Don't make it more difficult to say goodnight than it already is," he added with deliberate emphasis. "We have tomorrow."

A thought crowded into Joanna's mind that she had dismissed earlier. "But what about Dr. Eden? She's here to see you."

"She doesn't mean anything to me, Jo. She's a colleague. A friend."

"Like I'm your friend?" Joanna asked, her eyes wide with sudden anguish.

"No, no. It's nothing like that." He studied her uncertain gaze, wishing he could undo some of his past. "Joanna, there's no one like you in my life. No one." He paused. "And I'm tired of this senseless lying to myself."

Joanna frowned. "Lying? About what?"

"About not wanting you. I know you're too young for me and you have a serious faith in God that I don't yet share. But the truth is, no matter what our differences, I do want you. Only God knows how much." Jake's fingers were warm against her skin as he traced the line of her jaw.

Want was not the same as *love,* Joanna knew all too well; but the tender light in his eyes assured her it was a beginning. For now, that was enough.

"Tomorrow?" he reminded before leaning forward, his lips brushing hers in barely a kiss.

She laughed softly, stealing a second light kiss before she turned to leave. "Tomorrow," she repeated. Something Jake had not given until now. The promise of tomorrow.

"Good morning, Ina!" Joanna's voice, light and happy, brought an immediate frown to her friend's face early the next day.

"You're certainly cheerful this morning," Ina remarked as she poured steaming coffee into two mugs.

"And why shouldn't I be?" Joanna slipped her arms around Ina, giving her a hug. "It's a beautiful day, and I'm in love with a wonderful man." The smile lighting up Joanna's face did nothing to alleviate the frown on Ina's.

"In love? What are you talking about? Things couldn't have gone that well on a first date with…what was his name? Bob?"

"No, you're right about that. But when I came home, Jake was waiting for me. Where is he this morning, anyway?"

"He left for the hospital about an hour ago. He said he wouldn't be gone long." Ina sank down onto a kitchen chair. "Tell me what happened."

"Well…" Joanna began as she joined her friend at the table. Reaching across the table, she squeezed

Ina's hand. "Jake really cares for me, Ina. More than I ever dreamed he would."

"I know he does, dear, but—"

"We're going out tonight. Just the two of us." Joanna paused at the wonder of her own words. "I can hardly believe he agreed to it."

"Well, I'm sure you'll enjoy that, but—"

"I've loved him for so long, Ina. You can't imagine how it feels to finally have some hope. I know I've always been jealous of Natalie Eden, but he said last night that she didn't mean anything to him."

"I'll bet he did," Ina interjected.

Joanna's heart skipped a beat. "Why would you say that?" she asked, not certain she wanted to hear the answer.

"I know that you're in love with him, sweetie. I've known that since the first time I saw you with him, but whatever Jake said to you last night…"

"What is it, Ina?" Joanna watched a deep frown settle over her friend's kind face. "What happened?"

"Before Jake left for the airport last night to pick up Dr. Eden, he got a phone call. I'd been upstairs with Mae and was just coming down to the kitchen to make some coffee when he was talking on the phone."

"With whom?"

"It turned out to be Daniel Vernon, one of Andrew's sons, on the phone." Ina placed a hand over her mouth momentarily in a thoughtful gesture. "Jake was too quiet, solemn. Maybe even sad. I'm not sure how to accurately describe it, but when I walked past him, he was ending the conversation. There was something about his expression that concerned me, so I asked if everything was all right.''

''And...he said...'' Joanna prompted.

''He said that nothing was right. Nothing. Then he told me that Natalie Eden is marrying Daniel Vernon.''

''Natalie Eden and Daniel Vernon? You're not serious.''

Ina nodded her head.

''Daniel's a good friend of Jake's. I've heard Jake talk about him.'' She eased slowly into a chair. Her throat tightened, and being ill was becoming a real possibility. How wrong had her judgment been about Jake's feelings last night? Wrong enough to last a lifetime? ''So, news of the marriage...upset him?''

''I think so.'' Ina sighed. ''Believe me, if I didn't think this was important, I wouldn't mention it. I'm not one for gossiping. Honestly.'' Ina reached over to pat Joanna's hand. ''But he said he almost couldn't believe he felt this way. I told him if he wanted to talk, I'd be glad to listen. But he said he didn't have anything to say except that he was jealous of Daniel. Jealous. He repeated it as if he didn't believe what he was saying.''

''Jealous of Daniel Vernon,'' Joanna barely whispered. ''Because Daniel is marrying Natalie.''

''I'm afraid so,'' Ina answered as she gave Joanna's arm a gentle squeeze. ''He went storming out of here, slamming the door behind him. I've known Jake for years, and I've never seen him tear out of the driveway the way he did then.''

Joanna rose from her chair, pulling away from the

comforting touch of her friend to walk to the window. The brilliant sunshine did nothing to ease the sorrow that gripped her aching heart.

"Maybe he was jealous of your date with Bob, too. Do you think—"

"No," Joanna responded with certainty. "Jake knew it was a first date. It was nothing to be jealous of." But...all the things he'd said last night? Had he meant any of it? Or was she a convenient replacement for the woman he really longed for?

"But you showed interest in another man. Jake's not used to that kind of behavior from you. He's had you all to himself since you moved here."

"As though he's noticed," Joanna commented. "The only reason he was suddenly so interested in me last night was because he knew Natalie was gone. Really gone. He's too close a friend to Daniel to pursue her, regardless of how strong his feelings are for her." Joanna shrugged hopelessly. "And why shouldn't Jake be in love with her? She's gorgeous, intelligent, successful, wealthy." Joanna raised a hand to her forehead. "She's right for Jake, you know. She even *looks* right for him. They'd make a perfect set. Matching good looks, medical careers and bank accounts. I think they'd be very happy together."

"Jake belongs with you. Permanently," Ina stated matter-of-factly. "But, he might have to get her out of his system first. Sometimes that's how it is, Joanna, whether we like it or not."

Joanna blinked hard. The familiar burn of rising tears returned. She'd cried over Jake. Too many times. She had no desire to do it again. "Excuse me, Ina. I have to get ready to go to work."

"Joanna, wait. I'm sorry I had to tell you all this. I heard Jake come home late last night, but I had no idea he was downstairs when you came in. I didn't realize—"

"That I'd fallen conveniently into his empty arms?" Joanna finished the sentence with a weak laugh. "Well, I had. Again. The funny thing is, it feels so right, Ina. I can hardly believe that he wasn't sincere."

"I know he cares for you, dear, but he was just so angry."

"He was angry at first," Joanna remembered, "but he was so...so tender. He can be so gentle with me, Ina." She stopped abruptly, hugging her arms to her stomach. How could what she felt last night not be real?

"I'm sorry, Joanna. I had no idea you'd come down here this morning so excited."

"He said he didn't feel anything for Natalie. And I believed him...I trusted him."

"Talk to him about this. I don't believe for a second that he would do anything to hurt you."

"But everything that happened, all the things he said...how could he have feelings for her and say those words to me?"

"There has to be some misunderstanding," Ina insisted.

"I love Jake," Joanna admitted, "and last night I thought he was beginning to love me, too. That's the only misunderstanding."

"I know he cares very much for you, Joanna. There's a reasonable explanation for all of this."

"Can you think of one?"

"I'm trying," Ina acknowledged. "Even if he has some feelings for Dr. Eden, they won't last forever."

"And since he can't have her, he'll settle for me? No, Ina, I don't want him unless he loves me—only me."

"Don't let your pride get in the way. Discuss this with him. Tell the man you love him."

"Not now," Joanna said with a sad shrug. "What would I say when he tells me he doesn't feel the same?"

"You need to hear the truth, whatever it is. There are going to be things you're going to have to accept. Jake is a man who has made mistakes that need to be forgiven—just like the rest of us," Ina explained.

"Forgiveness has nothing to do with this. We're talking about believing in someone, trusting him…something a relationship can't survive without."

Ina rose from her chair to approach her young friend. She pressed a warm hand to Joanna's cheek. "What we're talking about is a lovely young woman whose pride has been hurt. If you love him, talk to him."

"Ina, it's not that simple," Joanna argued.

"I know, dear, but you're not being fair to him until you give him a chance to explain." She smiled at Joanna's troubled expression and tilted her head a little to the side. "Don't be afraid of what he has to say."

"But I am afraid, Ina. What do I have to really call my own? No family, no home...and now, Jake? I can't share his love with some woman from his past."

"Then give him a chance to explain her away."

Joanna quietly considered the words Ina had spoken, but nothing sounded logical in a moment when the only thing she could do was feel. "All I want to do is leave. Now. Today," she said. "I've prayed about this so many times, and the answer has always seemed to be wait, wait a little longer, until the time is right. But, now, I think the answer is no...not Jake...not for me."

She looked up to see the color drain from Ina's face in an instant. Joanna turned, knowing instinctively what had happened. And she was right. Jake stood silently in the doorway, his eyes fixed on Joanna.

"Excuse me," Ina mumbled and cast an encouraging look in Joanna's direction. "I need to check on Mae again. She wasn't doing well this morning," she added before she hurried from the kitchen.

Stone-cold silence settled over the room as Joanna placed both hands on the back of a nearby chair to steady herself. Her mind raced with thoughts. What had she said? How much had he heard? "Jake—"

"You would leave?" He spoke slowly with a lethal calmness keeping whatever emotion he was feeling in check. "Without discussion? Without explanation?"

"I wouldn't go without telling you."

"Telling me what? Goodbye?"

Joanna looked at him, the cautious gray of his eyes. The truth, Ina had said. But how could they get to it beneath all of the emotion? "You know Natalie Eden is marrying Daniel," she stated, her voice shaky.

Jake studied her questioning gaze. "Yes."

"You're not surprised by that?"

"No," Jake answered. "Daniel has been in love with her since our first year of medical school."

"But she's interested in you. Back in Charleston, you traveled to conferences with her, you dated her—"

"We went to dinner a few times. She's a friend, Joanna, someone I worked with."

Like I'm your friend. The words screamed through Joanna's mind, but she didn't speak them. He'd only deny it like he had last night. "So, then, will you be attending their wedding?" she asked, ignoring the swell of pain rising in her chest.

"No," Jake responded quietly. Not after the events of this morning's conversation. "I won't be going."

Joanna bit her lip until it throbbed. "Wise decision," she remarked crisply. "Then you don't have to worry about whether or not to take me along. I'm sure it would be quite an embarrassment. Being seen with the immature, frivolous twenty-two-year-old that I am."

"That's not true," he countered, swallowing the despair in his throat. He'd be the envy of every man there if he showed up at that ceremony with anyone as young and beautiful as Joanna on his arm. And standing in that solemn sanctuary, watching Daniel make eternal vows... Jake exhaled a quiet sigh. He'd want to ask Joanna to marry him. Like he wanted to do only moments ago... And he wasn't going to let

208 Heart of a Husband

that happen. Not when so slight a misunderstanding could send her fleeing. Running from him, without so much as a question asked. Just as his mother had done. "Believe me, Jo. It's not you. It's me. I can't go to that ceremony. It's not something I can do."

"I see," she answered softly, then locked her fingers together in prayerlike fashion, clasping her fidgeting hands in front of her. She felt Jake's eyes follow her movement.

"You're not going to pray now, are you?" he asked.

"What are you talking about?"

Jake nodded toward her hands. "I know that you're concerned about doing what is right for you, but I don't think this is an appropriate time for prayer."

Anger burned through her, one emotion she rarely experienced with him. "Don't make fun of me, Jake."

"I'm not," he replied immediately. "I wouldn't do anything to stand in the way of your Christianity, Jo, but I don't want to find myself standing in the middle of it."

"Because you won't accept it."

"Because I don't fully understand it," he said. "I haven't misled you." He thought they had at least reached an understanding on that obstacle. "You know that I don't share your beliefs—you've known that from the beginning." He paused. "You knew that last night."

Joanna stiffened at the sting of hurtful words. She had always known but, somehow, she had still hoped. "Yes, I guess I did, didn't I?" she lamented. "And, as I recall, you seemed quite sure last night that Natalie Eden didn't mean anything to you.''

"Because she doesn't," Jake answered, a flash of anger burning through his own gaze. "I've told you that. Why won't you believe me?"

"And yet you won't watch her marry Daniel."

"I don't care who Natalie marries. I'm not in the mood to go to anyone's wedding," he said in a clipped, tense voice. Least of all, his own.

Joanna's brown eyes clung to his in a desperate search for some glimpse of the tenderness she'd seen only hours earlier. But it was gone. "If you'll excuse me, I have some packing to do before I leave for work." She took a few steps toward the doorway and Jake stepped aside to let her pass. How quickly and easily this was ending. She'd never imagined it being like this.

"Joanna." The unfamiliar tone in his voice stopped her. He sounded so cold, so clinical. "Mae is staying here where she can be taken care of properly. You will explain your departure to her in some way that makes sense."

She gave a forced smile. "Yes, I'll talk to her." Was that all he had to say? Didn't he care at all that she was leaving?

"The decision to go is yours to make. You know what's right for you," he stated, "but when you leave, I want to be informed where I can reach you."

A cry of exasperation escaped her. "You don't have to look after me, Jake. I'm quite capable of taking care of myself, thank you."

"I realize that," he answered, his voice sounding

oddly resigned, "but if you're not living here, you still need to be nearby. I promised Mae that you would be here for her." His mouth took an unpleasant twist of determination. "I intend to keep that promise."

"Yes, keep your promise to Aunt Mae," she said in clear, cool words. "That's what started this whole situation, isn't it?"

"We started it ourselves, Jo, by wanting things we cannot have."

Joanna watched the play of emotions on his face. Whatever Jake wanted was more unclear to her now than ever, but she'd learned exactly what she wanted. The love she'd begun to believe in last night. How could she have been so wrong? Turning, she left the kitchen and rushed up the stairs to her bedroom. The truth they needed was buried somewhere in the words they'd spoken to each other. It had to be there. If only they could find their way to it.

She pulled her suitcases from the closet and dropped them onto the bed as the first of many tears slid down her cheeks. But the yanking of sweaters and blouses from hangers and stuffing them haphazardly into the luggage stopped abruptly at the sound of Ina's panicked voice.

"Joanna, come quick!"

She ran into the hallway, nearly colliding with her friend. "Is it Aunt Mae?" Joanna asked, running toward her aunt's room down the long hallway.

"Where's Dr. Barnes?" the nurse asked as she was coming out of the doorway just as Joanna rushed in.

Ina was by Joanna's side in an instant, slipping an

arm gently around her waist. Mae was gone. Peacefully, quickly, gone. And she'd taken what was left of Joanna's heart with her that day.

The funeral was brief. Simple and fitting. Aunt Mae was buried in a small country cemetery only a few miles from Jake's home. She had been born and raised less than fifty miles from that spot so Joanna gave no argument when Jake suggested it as a final resting place. His father was buried there, Joanna noticed when she inspected the area with Ina to see if it was acceptable. But there'd been only one tombstone with the Barnes name on it. She wondered briefly why Jake's mother was buried elsewhere. Wouldn't any woman have wanted to been laid to rest alongside her husband if it was possible? Mae's husband had been cremated years ago. Otherwise, Joanna would have requested her aunt's body be shipped home to be buried beside her uncle. She couldn't imagine choosing otherwise for herself. If Jake had loved her... But he didn't, she reminded herself, and there wasn't any point in considering possibilities that had never really existed.

It wasn't Jake's shoulder Joanna cried on during those difficult days. Ina was her mainstay for what little weeping she did. She felt more numb than sad, and she longed for the familiarity of the home she had shared with Mae, a house she would have to sell immediately to pay bills. Returning to Charleston as soon as Smithfield found someone to replace her, was her plan. In the meantime, she moved temporarily into Ina's home in a subdivision near the city. With Aunt

Mae gone, Ina wasn't needed at Jake's home as much so she, along with Joanna, packed their things and moved. Jake let them go with little more than a nod goodbye. And Joanna was glad. It made the leaving easier. As did the news from Andrew Vernon that the marriage between his son and Dr. Natalie Eden had been called off. It seemed the couple couldn't agree whether home would be Indiana or South Carolina. The engagement was over and Dr. Eden had returned to the clinic in Charleston. Alone. For now, at least. Joanna felt that she herself had accepted the news rather well, considering her prediction had come true. Jake would be gone for good with Natalie available again, and Joanna didn't shed a single tear over that knowledge. In fact, she took her small paycheck from Smithfield and went shopping. But not even two new pairs of shoes and a shiny silver locket eased the persistent ache within. If the lovely Dr. Eden had been trying to make Dr. Barnes jealous with news of an engagement, she'd certainly succeeded. And the payoff would probably be a lifetime with him.

Joanna sighed. Sliding the shoe boxes into the bedroom closet, she lay back on the bed. It was over. Whatever misguided notion she'd had that she might have a future with Jake had ended. He didn't want marriage, he had said. But he'd change his mind or, rather, Natalie Eden would change it for him. And Joanna didn't want to be around to see it when it happened.

"At least I didn't tell him I love him," she said to herself in the stillness of the bedroom. "Thank you, Lord, for saving me from that embarrassment." But she'd felt strongly impressed to say it. More than once. And what good would it have done?

No, she'd done the right thing, the only thing that made sense. She'd kept her mouth shut, her heart closed and walked away with what little pride she had left. She'd lost more than her hope for the future when she'd left Jake's home. She lost the friend that he'd been. And her pride wasn't a comforting companion.

Tears flooded her eyes. ''Lord, what am I going to do now? Aunt Mae's gone, Jake's as good as gone....'' She'd never felt so alone in all her life.

''I will never leave thee, nor forsake thee.'' The scripture verse came to mind. ''Never leave thee, never leave thee.'' There was no love like God's in all the world. Joanna was certain of it. And it was the only love that held true. The only love that remained. She eased off her bed and onto her knees as raw grief overwhelmed her. She would ask the Lord for clarity in the midst of the confusion of her ever changing life. He was the only place left to go.

Chapter Twelve

The ringing phone in the office at Smithfield caught Joanna's attention as she was lining up the children for play rehearsal. She grabbed up the phone quickly.

"Joanna? This is Ina. I'm having car trouble."

"Okay, hold on a minute." Joanna moved the receiver away from her ear. "Kids," she said loudly over the chatter of the children standing outside the office door. "Stay right where you are until I'm finished with this call." Then she was back on the phone. "Car trouble? Do you want me to pick you up?"

"Could you? What time are you leaving work?" Ina asked.

Joanna glanced up at a nearby clock on the wall. "In about half an hour. But I promised to take Aaron to the mall to help me buy some things for the play, so I'll have to bring him with me. Where are you?"

"I had some cleaning to do today. I'm at Dr. Barnes's house."

"Ina, are you really having car trouble, or is this some sort of trick to get me over there to see Jake?"

"Dr. Barnes isn't even here. Is it my fault that my car gave out on me in his driveway? Now, can you pick me up, or not?"

"I'll be there, but not for about an hour."

"Okay, see you then, dear," Ina replied, and although Joanna was unable to see it, Ina had a sly grin on her face as she hung up the receiver.

"That's Doc's car!" Aaron exclaimed when Joanna pulled into the familiar driveway less than an hour later and parked beside Jake's silver automobile.

"Yep! That's his car, Jo-Jo!" Aaron repeated as he unfastened his seat belt and climbed out of the car.

"Thanks a lot, Ina," Joanna mumbled under her breath while getting out of the vehicle. It had been two weeks since she'd seen Jake, and although Ina continued to work for him several days a week, Joanna had refused to even discuss Jake with Ina. Joanna needed to forget him, and thinking about him was not the way to do it.

"Thanks for coming, Joanna," Ina called to her as she came out of the front door, "but we seem to have the car running now. I guess there wasn't anything seriously wrong with it."

"The question is, was there ever anything wrong with it at all?" Joanna asked while watching Aaron run up the front steps to ring the doorbell.

"Now, would I lie?" Ina replied without looking at Joanna. She pulled open the door to her older model car and set her purse on the front seat. "I told you Dr. Barnes wasn't here when I called, and he wasn't."

"No, but I'll bet you knew exactly when he would arrive—just a few minutes before me."

Ina laughed and winked at her. "Go inside and say hello to him, Joanna. He hasn't been himself since we moved out, and I don't think it's my departure that has made him so irritable."

"Doc!" Aaron exclaimed when Jake stepped out onto the front porch.

"Hi, Aaron!" Jake replied, and he leaned down to give the boy a big hug. "How are you, champ? I've missed you."

"I like that name. Champ. Nobody calls me that but you," Aaron said. "I tell my friends that's what Doc calls me."

Jake laughed and clasped Aaron's small hand in his own. They walked down the wide front steps.

Joanna bit her lower lip firmly. Jake's laughter. Not until this moment did she realize how much she missed that sound.

"Hello," he said when their eyes met. The thin line of his mouth straightened. The smile was gone.

"Hello, Jake. How are you?" she asked, more glad for the sight of him than she wanted to admit.

Before Jake could answer, Aaron asked in an excited voice, "I'm gonna be in a play Friday night. Can you come?"

"I don't know. I'm going to be in South Carolina for a few days for a conference."

"Charleston?" Joanna regretted the question almost before it slipped out.

Jake's eyes locked with hers for a brief moment. "Yes, for a conference," he repeated.

But Joanna knew there was more than a conference awaiting Jake in Charleston.

"What time on Friday, champ?" Jake returned his attention to the little boy.

"Seven and a half."

"Seven-thirty, Aaron," Joanna gently corrected.

"Yes, that's it. Seven-thirty."

Jake's broad smile warmed Joanna's heart, and she had to look away from him for fear he might read her feelings in her eyes. She watched as Ina started her car, pulled away from the driveway and glanced back at Joanna with a nod of satisfaction. Ina's mission had been accomplished. She had gotten them together again. At least they were talking, although Joanna wished they weren't.

"My flight is scheduled to arrive at six-thirty that evening, so I'll be there unless there's a delay."

"Did you hear that, Jo-Jo? Doc's gonna come see me in my play!"

"Yes, I heard. That's very nice of him, isn't it, Aaron?" She was speaking to the child at her side, but her gaze now lingered on the man standing close to her on the driveway.

"My pleasure," Jake responded. "Maybe I could have a reserved seat somewhere close to the front," he added, the silver-gray of his eyes filled with warmth.

She swallowed at the lump in her throat. "One seat or two?" she asked, remembering Charleston.

He looked away. "I don't think this is something I should invite someone to. Do you?"

"No, I suppose not," Joanna said, dissatisfied with his evasive reply though she knew she deserved it.

Jake turned his attention to Aaron and tousled the youngster's hair gently. "So, you're in this play?"

"Yep. Jo-Jo is making me be in it, but it will be fun now that you're comin', Doc."

"We'd better get going, Aaron," Joanna said. "We have some shopping to do, and I'm supposed to have you back in time for dinner."

"See ya!" Aaron called to Jake as he ran toward the car, pulled open the door and climbed into the front seat.

Jake waved at the boy, then transferred his gaze to Joanna. "So, I'll see you Friday evening at seven and a half," he said with a hint of a smile tugging at the corners of his mouth.

Joanna smiled. "Thanks for agreeing to come to this play. It means a lot to him."

"I'll enjoy being there. He's a special kid, Jo."

She nodded her head in agreement and fumbled nervously with the car keys in her hand. "I hope you have a good time at the conference."

"That would be a first," he remarked. "I have yet to have a good time at a conference."

Joanna wished she could believe him. Glancing toward the automobile again, she shook her head at Aaron when he blew the horn impatiently. "Well, have a safe trip. We'll see you Friday."

"Goodbye," she heard him say as she turned and walked away, feeling as though she had left a portion of her heart right there on the driveway with Jake. Seeing him again was every bit as difficult as she had feared it would be, and she dreaded the arrival of Friday evening. But as she drove down the road with the excited chatter of Aaron beside her, she began to feel a little of the heaviness within her heart ease.

"You're a good companion, Aaron," Joanna commented.

"Com-pan-yun... What's that, Jo-Jo?"

"Someone to be with, a friend," Joanna explained in simple terms.

"Thanks. You, too," Aaron replied. "Doc, too."

"Yes," Joanna whispered sadly. "Doc, too."

The days flew by and before anyone was completely ready for the spring play performance, it was here. Friday night. Curtain time.

A good crowd of foster parents, friends and volunteers had shown up for the children's play, and Joanna was zipping up the back of Freddie's sunflower costume when Ina came into the backstage dressing room.

"Everything looks great, Joanna."

"Who are you?" Freddie demanded, pushing several large yellow artificial petals from his face.

"Be polite, Freddie," Joanna scolded. "What should you say to our visitor?"

"Uh...what's your name, ma'am?" Freddie shrugged his shoulders as he struggled for the correct response.

"Close enough," Joanna said, and she snapped shut the safety pin at the back of his costume. "This is Mrs. Marsh, a good friend of mine, and Mrs. Marsh, this is Freddie.''

"A good friend of yours, too, Jo-Jo," Freddie added emphatically.

"Yes, you are. Now, hurry up and tie your other shoe, or you're going to be late for your entrance."

"See ya, Mrs. Marsh," Freddie said as he stooped to tie his shoelaces.

"I think we're nearly ready. Thanks for coming, Ina."

"Are you kidding? I wouldn't miss this for the world. Seeing these little kids in their costumes is going to be fun."

"I hope so," Joanna said with a sigh. "It's almost time. Is Jake here yet?"

"I don't think so."

"Aaron will be so disappointed if he doesn't come."

"I don't think Aaron will be the only one," Ina commented. She peeked around the stage curtain. "I'll go see if I can find him in the crowd. There are a lot of people out here, you know."

"There should be a couple of seats in the second row for you and Jake. I left my sweater on the back of one chair, and there's a stack of programs on the other one."

Ina disappeared around the corner, walking toward the chairs and keeping a watchful eye on the crowd in search of Jake.

Remembering she needed a couple of extra programs for backstage, Joanna went out to the seats she had reserved to retrieve them. That's when Ina heard a woman who had just entered the room mention a problem at the airport.

Ina touched the woman's arm gently. "Excuse me, what were you saying about the airport?"

"There's been a plane crash. About an hour ago," she replied.

Ina glanced down at her watch. It was nearly seven-thirty. Jake's flight had been scheduled to come in at six-thirty. "Which plane? How serious is it?" Ina deluged the woman with questions. "Where did the flight come from?"

"I'm sorry, but I really don't know many of the details. I only heard the news bulletin about a flight from somewhere down south."

"Oh, no." Ina's hand flew to her mouth. "Jake." She turned toward the front of the auditorium, looking for Joanna. The news spread through the crowd like wildfire, and Ina knew she had to get to Joanna before someone else told her. She knew Joanna had lost her parents in a plane crash, and now...

There were lots of flights from the south. Ina rehearsed the words she would say. *Atlanta, Miami, Tampa...* That doesn't mean it was Jake's plane. She worked her way through the rush of people, wanting to reach Joanna before this news did.

But Ina did not get there in time.

Chapter Thirteen

"No...no..." Joanna said in a hushed tone. "This can't be happening...it can't."

Ina pushed through the mingling crowd toward the front of the auditorium where Joanna was standing. By the time Ina reached her, she was shouting.

"No! Not Jake!" She reached frantically for her purse through streaming tears, knocking over a stack of programs from the chair beside her. "Car keys. Where are my car keys?" she mumbled under her breath.

"Joanna, honey," Ina said as she touched her shoulder. "We don't know which flight it was. I'm sure Jake's all right."

"Don't, Ina." Joanna jerked away from her. Dumping the contents of her purse onto the floor, she grabbed up her keys and rose to her feet.

"Joanna, you can't go out there."

But she did not respond to Ina as she hurried away from her, through the mass of people and confusion toward the side exit. Bursting into the cold night air, she bolted for her car located on the far side of the parking lot.

"Joanna!" Ina trailed behind her, calling her name. "Wait! Wait for me!"

"Not Jake. Please don't let it be Jake, Lord. Please, please, please." Through her tears, Joanna couldn't find the correct key and her fumbling fingers allowed Ina time to catch up with her just as she slid the key into the lock.

Ina gripped Joanna's arm, but Joanna yanked free of her. "I'm going out to that airport to find him."

"All right. If you must go, at least let me drive," Ina insisted.

"No. Go back inside, Ina." Joanna jerked open the car door.

But Ina pushed her way in front of Joanna and climbed into the driver's side. "You're crying too hard to even see. Now, quit arguing and get in the other side."

Joanna quickly climbed into the passenger seat without argument and buried her face in her hands. She was sobbing uncontrollably as Ina backed out of the parking space and guided the car onto the highway.

"Honey, calm down. Jake will be fine," Ina assured her, and at the same time wished she could believe her own words.

"No, he's not. He's late. He should have been here by now." Joanna coughed from all the crying. "Oh, God, I can't stand it if I've lost him."

Ina blinked hard, holding back her own threatening tears. "Now, Joanna, he's been late so many times, it doesn't mean that he's hurt. He's a doctor and if people were injured, he'd be there helping."

"He'd let me know. If he's okay, he'd let me know. He knows Mom and Dad died in a plane—" but her voice broke into a sob before she could finish.

"If he's helping injured passengers, he couldn't take time out to make a telephone call, honey." Ina looked both ways and proceeded to run a red light.

"Can't you drive any faster?" Joanna asked.

"I'm trying to be careful. If I get you hurt out here on this highway, I'd never forgive myself," Ina replied.

"It doesn't matter." Joanna's sobs grew louder. She pulled her legs up, hugging her knees to her chest and wished for the pain that ripped through her heart to stop. "All that matters is Jake. I don't want him to die. I'd rather it be me than him."

"Don't say that. Everything is going to be fine. You'll see."

But when they started down the long entrance road to the airport, everything did not look fine. Red lights flashed from vehicles virtually everywhere.

"Oh, no," Joanna choked out as she leaned forward.

A policeman waved them off the road. Ina rolled down her window to explain.

"No way, lady," the office stated flatly. "Too much happening here. You'll have to move your car, be on your way."

"Go home, Ina," Joanna ordered. Then she opened the car door and ran, cutting across the grass toward the main building before Ina realized what was happening.

"Hey! Stop that woman!" one officer yelled to another one farther up the roadway. And the second officer reached for her, catching her by the arm as she attempted to run past him. Ina held her breath as she watched Joanna twist free of his grasp and run to the main entrance.

"Good girl," Ina spoke aloud to herself. "Now, go find him and, please, please, Lord, let him be there, safe, for her to find."

Joanna entered the lobby, slipping past several security guards and working her way through the crowd. Several cots leaned against one of the walls and there were people, many of them weeping, throughout the hallway. Joanna held her hand up to her eyes and squinted, hoping to catch at least a glimpse of what was going on outside the plate glass windows along the back of the lobby. But her view was blocked by various police officers and a natural partition of shrubbery.

The board displaying the flight schedules caught Joanna's attention, and she looked up at the list of departure and arrival times. None of the information displayed helped because she did not know which airline he had taken. Looking away from the useless schedule, she noticed an employee behind the ticket counter nearest her.

"Excuse me," she said, not caring that she was interrupting the woman's telephone conversation. Other phone lines were ringing and lights flashed with calls left temporarily on hold. "Can you help me? I'm looking for a doctor. His name is Jake Barnes, and I'm not sure which flight—"

"Are you injured?" the woman asked as she cradled the telephone receiver between her ear and shoulder.

"No, he's a passenger. His name is—"

"Which flight number?"

"I don't know. I'm afraid it was—" Joanna couldn't finish the sentence because of the sob that caught in her throat.

"I'm sorry, miss, but I can't help you now. Have a seat over there, and let me take care of these calls. Then maybe I can find out something for you." The woman nodded her head toward the chairs in the center of the lobby.

Joanna turned to see dozens of people seated, some alone, others sat in couples, waiting. Tears spilled over her lashes and trickled down her face. "No," she said, "I can't just sit and wait."

"You'll have to," the woman replied firmly.

"But the plane that crashed, where did it come from?"

"The flight originated in Miami, but made several stops along the way. Please have a seat, miss."

"But, the accident, it's bad, isn't it?" Joanna persisted.

"I really don't have all the details. I'll tell you more when I know."

Joanna tucked several strands of hair behind an ear and returned her gaze to the waiting people in the lobby, people who had apparently arrived to pick up a friend or a loved one coming in on that plane. Now they were waiting to see whether or not that person was safe. Joanna did not want to be counted among them. She wanted Jake to be alive and well, and she wanted that more dearly than she wanted to draw her next breath.

She sank onto one of the plastic orange chairs, pulling her feet up and hugging her legs to her. Resting her chin on her knees, she whispered, "Please, Lord, don't let me lose him like this. Not like this. Please." Then she had a glimmer of hope. Maybe he'd stayed in Charleston. Natalie Eden would be reason enough for him to spend an extra day there. Maybe he was safe in South Carolina with no knowledge that this accident had even taken place. But she doubted it. He'd told Aaron he would be here for the play if he could, and Jake was a man of his word. This would probably be the only time in life she'd ever regret that quality in him. There was nothing left to do but pray and wait.

Ina had been right. She should have told Jake she loved him from the beginning. He had a right to know. She could have told him. But, no, she had been too proud, too jealous, too afraid of his response. And, why? She knew Jake cared for her, very much. She was suddenly certain of it. She'd seen it in his tenderness, felt it in his touch. Maybe he could learn to love her the way she loved him.

And, what if he did? There was no way they could build a life together without a solid foundation. What if he wouldn't accept her faith? What if he chose to never love God? What if he'd left this world tonight without loving God? Her mind raced with thoughts, bits and pieces of what might have been, what could still be.

"I'll do whatever you ask of me, Lord," Joanna

whispered. "Just please, please, don't let him die now. Not like this. Don't let it be like this."

Time seemed to lose all meaning as Joanna remained curled up in the chair, praying silently as she waited. Until a familiar voice sliced through the confusion surrounding her.

"Joanna? Dear girl, what are you doing here?"

Andrew Vernon's voice jolted her.

She jumped up immediately. "Where's Jake? Is he with you, Andrew?"

"Jake? No, I came over here from the hospital as soon as I heard about the accident. I've only been here a few minutes."

"Oh, Andrew, I think Jake was on that plane...I think he's..."

"No!" Andrew exclaimed. "No, no, that can't be right."

Joanna clutched a handful of his jacket in her fists. Shrugging her shoulders, she nodded her head through her tears. "I think...oh, God, I think I've lost him."

"No, now, don't you cry," Andrew said. "You sit back down here, and I'll find out what's going on."

"Can you? Will you?" Joanna held tightly to his jacket, her knees weakening.

"Yes, I'll find him. Now, sit down." Andrew gripped her arms in an effort to support her, but she pulled away from him, sinking to the floor. Folding her arms on the seat of the chair, she buried her face in her arms. "Hurry, Andrew. Hurry, please, hurry."

Andrew touched her shoulder and then disappeared into the restricted area that only emergency personnel were permitted to enter. Joanna's breaking heart went virtually unnoticed in the rush of people desperate for information that was slow in coming. She pulled her shirt free from her jeans and wiped repeatedly at the steady flow of tears, but to no avail. They were falling faster than she could dry them. If only she could have him back again, have another chance.

"Please, don't take him now, Lord. Not now when he's so far from You. He's not ready. And I know that wanting a lifetime with a man who doesn't love You isn't right for me. But he's been my friend for years—a friend I love. If that's all we ever have, it will be enough for me. I promise to stay within whatever boundaries you set for me. Just, please, don't let me lose him now. Not now."

Two medics came rushing in from the airfield pushing a cart transporting a young pregnant woman, obviously in labor. They moved toward the front of the area where several emergency vehicles had been stationed earlier. Joanna was rubbing her reddened eyes or she would have seen the doctor accompanying the young woman. His clothing was stained with a mixture of dirt and spattered blood, and he was answering the questions of the woman's worried husband as they followed closely behind the cart. But as he spoke, he scanned the lobby until his eyes rested on Joanna's huddled form in the far corner.

"We'll need to wait a minute for the next ambulance. Stay with the medics."

"But, doctor?" the young husband protested as Jake walked away.

"One minute. That's all I need. Stay with your wife," Jake ordered as he began making his way through the crowd.

Joanna pulled herself up onto the chair, wiped at the side of her face with her shirtsleeve and looked out toward the hallway into which Andrew had disappeared.

"Joanna! Jo!"

She jumped up from her seat. She'd heard Jake's voice, she thought. But, where?

Then he stepped through the crowd of people that had been blocking Joanna's view.

"Jake! Oh, thank God, it's you!" Joanna flew into his arms, laughing and crying, sobbing and hugging. "Dear God, thank you. You're alive, you're all right! Are you all right?" She saw the blood on the front of his shirt.

"Yes, I'm okay. I'm all right." His arms tightened around her, his mouth pressing to her temple. "I'm sorry you were frightened."

"Oh, Jake, I was so afraid. I thought I'd lost you. I thought—"

"I know." He held her close, breathing in the fragrance of her. "Andrew told me."

"Thank God, you're alive. Thank you, thank you, thank you," she whispered against his chest as she clung to him, never wanting to let him out of her sight again.

"It wasn't my flight, Jo. I tried to get a message to you. I knew you'd hear about the crash, and it would remind you of your parents." Jake kissed the top of her head before he pulled back. Then his hands gently cupped her face, bringing her gaze up to his.

"I thought you were gone," she cried. "How could I go through all the years without you?"

"It's all right, I'm here, I'm okay." He searched

her watery eyes, wondering where to start with all he needed to say.

"I realize I—" Joanna began, convinced that if she didn't speak her mind now, she might never again find the courage "—I can't have you, Jake. Not the way I want to, but...I'm so in love with you...."

"Honey, I know. I knew that before you did," he admitted in no more than a husky whisper.

"But the past doesn't matter." She wiped a smudge of dirt from his cheekbone. "Can't we leave it behind and, at least, still be friends? I love you too much to lose that, too."

"Joanna..." Jake stopped, his voice wavering with emotion. Tears burned his eyes.

"It's okay," she whispered, her heart breaking from the response he didn't give. "You don't need to say anything. I understand."

"Understand that I love you, Jo. I've loved you for such a long time," came his words as tenderly as she had imagined.

"Jake, oh, Jake!" she cried. Her arms flew around his neck as he leaned forward, his mouth claiming hers in the sweetest of kisses.

But red flashing lights pulsated through the huge glass entryway, bringing their shared moment to an end.

"There's the ambulance," he said as he glanced through the windows. Then he looked back into her shimmering eyes. "There are so many things I need to tell you. Come with me." Jake reluctantly pulled away from her but clasped her hand firmly in his own.

"Where are we going?"

"To the hospital with this couple. I told them I'd only be away for a minute."

Joanna was led through the crowd to the doorway where the ambulance was backing up toward the building. Jake continued to hold tightly to Joanna's hand even as he spoke with paramedics and the young couple. Then he squeezed her fingers and motioned to an idle taxi parked several yards away. "You'll need to take this cab."

While the paramedics loaded the patient into the emergency vehicle, Jake pulled some money from his wallet. "She needs to go to St. Luke's—the ER entrance."

Joanna found it almost painful to let go of his hand.

"You'll be okay," he assured her with a light kiss. "I'll see you at the hospital."

She climbed into the cab, and Jake closed the door, giving her a quick wink before he walked away. Turning to look out of the side window, she watched him disappear into the back of the ambulance. Soon sirens blared and red lights flashed once again as they sped out of the airport parking lot, and the taxi followed slower behind them. Trees and lights from passing vehicles became a blur and in a surprisingly short time, the cabdriver pulled up to St. Luke's Hospital not too far behind the ambulance.

A sense of urgency enveloped everyone as the automatic doors of the emergency room opened and the patient was rushed inside the building. Joanna walked in a good distance behind the entourage, wanting to stay out of the way. Once she was inside the hospital, Joanna located the nearest telephone and quickly dialed Ina's number.

"Hello, Ina," she spoke into the receiver.

"Joanna? Are you all right? Did you find Jake?"

"Yes, we're both fine. We're at the hospital now and he's with a patient."

"But he's all right! Thank the Lord!" Ina exclaimed. "Are you going to stay at the hospital? Do you want me to come pick you up?"

"No, I'll wait for Jake," Joanna said quietly, suddenly overwhelmed with tiredness. "I don't want to leave without him."

"Stay with him as long as you need to, Joanna. I'll see you when you get home."

Joanna murmured a quick reply and replaced the receiver. Then she found the nearest ladies' room to wash her face. Her makeup was a disaster from crying, just as she'd known it would be. And her hair. She frowned at the reflection in the mirror. Working her fingers through her disheveled hair the best she could, she thought of her purse. Abandoned on the floor of the auditorium at Smithfield, along with her brush, lipstick and money. She now vividly recalled the panic that had clawed at her throat. Her head ached with the remembrance. Fresh air. That was what she needed.

Hurrying down the corridor, she escaped through the large sliding doors into the midnight air so refreshing and cool. The stars shone brilliantly from their depths in the black sky, and she wondered if she ever would have noticed them again, if she'd lost Jake tonight. And now that she had him back, safe and sound, and his love, how could she let him go? Wasn't that the promise she'd made? Not to give her future to a man who didn't love God?

The swoosh of the automatic doors opening caught her attention, and she turned her head to see Jake walking toward her.

"You okay?" he asked, a look of concern darkening his eyes.

"Yes." She smiled. How could she tell him what she'd promised? "Has your patient had her baby?"

"No, not yet," Jake answered, fatigue apparent in his solemn tone. "Dr. Stevens is here now, so they don't need me."

"But I do," she said softly. It had been true for so long, she could not remember when her need of him had begun.

When he smiled, some of his weariness faded, and she knew her words had pleased him more than he would say.

"I didn't think I'd ever hear you say that." His voice was quiet against the still of the evening as he stood facing her beneath the harsh lights of the emergency room entrance. Reaching out, he touched her hair.

Headlights flashed across them as a vehicle pulled into the archway covering the entrance.

"You're not going back to the airport, are you?" Joanna asked as they both looked toward the intruding car.

"No, they had things pretty well under control by the time Andrew arrived. That's the cab I called," Jake commented and he took Joanna's hand in his, lacing his fingers through hers. "Let's go home."

Home. For the last few weeks home had meant Ina's house. But Jake couldn't take her back to Ina's now, Joanna reasoned silently. Not when there was so much between them that needed to be said. Joanna unwittingly held her breath as the cabdriver asked their destination and, only after Jake responded with one address—his—did she breathe again.

Jake leaned back against the seat and stretched his legs out in the roomy back seat of the taxi.

Joanna turned to look into his eyes, only to find them filled with amusement.

"What's so funny?"

"Were you afraid that I would take you back to Ina's?" he asked. "Or that I wouldn't?"

"I want to be with you, Jake, but..." she began in a solemn tone and watched the humor fade from his expression.

"That's where you belong, Jo." He studied her wordlessly for a moment. "Your own room is still available, if that's what concerns you."

Nodding her head in silent acknowledgment, she slipped her arm through his and leaned her head on his shoulder. "I don't want to leave you so soon after finding you," she whispered. "Jake, I know you're a good man, but..."

"But that's not enough, is it?" Jake commented.

Joanna looked into those gray eyes that could sometimes so easily mask his emotion. "It's not enough for God. Tonight I kept thinking in the back of my mind that you weren't ready. That you haven't accepted the Lord, and I couldn't stand it, Jake," she admitted as she pulled away from him, wanting to convey the urgency of her words. "I really thought I had lost you in that plane crash tonight, and as much as I felt I couldn't live without you, even more I knew I couldn't face the thought of your lost soul. And it

would have been partly my fault. I could have done
more, said more—"

"Joanna—"

"You've got to do some serious thinking about
this, Jake. You need God in your life."

"Jo." He took her hand in his. "I've already
thought about it."

"Then you need to do something about it," she
insisted, not caring that the cabdriver was hearing
their entire conversation.

"I have," he replied. "Jo, if I had died in that
plane tonight, I'd be with the Lord right now. I
haven't done any work for Him, and there wouldn't
be rewards awaiting me, but at least I've taken care
of the basics."

"You've accepted Christ?" she exclaimed.

"As Lord and Savior of my life," he added with
a smile. His eyes, warm and tender, searched hers,
and he was not disappointed. He saw joy and love
smiling at him in return.

Instantly, she was in his arms. "I can hardly believe it! I'm so glad."

"So am I," he responded as he hugged her close,
his mouth moving against the softness of her hair.
"At the conference today I had lunch with several
other physicians. There were six of us seated at our
table and after the waitress brought our meals, two of
those men bowed their heads and thanked God for
their food." Jake paused as if to consider the wonder
of his own words. "Those two men prayed while I
sat there knowing I couldn't join them. I didn't know
this Lord they served. And I thought of you, and how
I've watched you pray before every meal I've ever

shared with you. You and those two men had something in your lives that I didn't have. And I wanted it, Joanna. In a way I never had before. So, I talked to them—like I talk to you—about church, faith, so many things. But it was their praying that stuck with me."

Joanna eased from his embrace, watching his expression of satisfaction as he spoke.

"I knew they had a relationship with their Creator that I didn't have. A relationship I wanted." Jake clasped her hand securely in his, squeezing it gently. "I skipped the afternoon lecture and went back to my hotel room to call your pastor."

"You called Pastor White? From South Carolina?"

"Yes, and he explained to me that I didn't need to be in a church to ask the Lord to forgive me, that I could do that where I was. So...I did." Jake's voice faltered, bringing fresh tears to Joanna's eyes.

"I'm so glad," she whispered, "So thankful."

"Look at this," he said, and he released her hand to reach into his pocket. "I bought this New Testament in the airport lobby in Charleston."

But his pocket was empty.

"Oh, that's right," he remembered, "I gave it to an injured man on the plane."

Joanna laughed softly. "You're a Christian for one day and already you're handing out scripture. You're off to a good start, don't you think?"

Jake laughed, too, and he stretched out his arm across the back of the seat. "C'mere," he said, pulling her closer. "Let me hold you."

With her head resting on his shoulder, Joanna

placed a hand on his chest, feeling the steady pounding of a peaceful heart beneath her palm.

"It's as though for the first time, I'm seeing things clearly. Christianity, life, love...you." The warmth of his mouth brushed her temple as he spoke. "But I couldn't do this for you, Joanna. I couldn't turn to God until I was ready," he said in a voice so still she barely heard it. "It had to be in my own time or not at all."

"I understand," Joanna replied. "That's the way it has to be for everyone."

"I'm thirty-four years old, Jo. That's a late start on this Christian way of life."

"It's not late," she protested. "You have your whole life ahead of you."

The cabdriver coughed loudly, reminding them they were not alone. They were leaving the city behind them, and Joanna looked out at the lights as they faded in the distance. The serenity of the country surrounded them, and only the headlights of the cab dispelled the darkness as they headed home.

"The plane crash—was it awful?" she asked.

"Not as bad as people were saying. I heard there was a problem with the landing gear. There were quite a few injuries, but most were minor. I was waiting on my luggage when I heard the news, so I stayed to do what I could." He paused. "I knew you'd be frightened when you heard, so I asked one of the women at the ticket counter to call you at Smithfield to give you a message."

"I left there in such a hurry after I heard about the accident, I didn't even think of checking at the front desk for messages."

"Poor Aaron," Jake said. "I hate letting him down."

"I know, and I did, too. I ran out of there without even thinking about the play. I hope Barbara and Bob got through it okay without me. I'll call when we get home to let Aaron know you're safe."

It was dark and quiet as they rode along. There were questions Joanna wanted to ask. Answers she needed.

"Jake," she began with uncertainty.

He needed only to look into her downcast expression to know exactly what troubled her.

She tried to continue, "I said that the past didn't matter—"

"Of course, it matters," he said and tenderly touched her cheek. "We'll talk when we get home."

Joanna nodded in agreement, and they rode in silence the remainder of the trip, content with the closeness they shared and the quiet time together those unanswered questions allowed.

Chapter Fourteen

The crisp night air was damp with the scent of rain that had fallen earlier in the day. Jake draped an arm around Joanna's shoulders as they watched the cab drive away. Then together they walked through the moonlight and stepped onto the porch.

"Why didn't you leave a light on?" Joanna asked.

Jake slid the key into the lock. Then he turned to her. "If I'd left one on, then I wouldn't be standing here in the dark with you now, would I?"

Joanna smiled, looking into the deep gray of his eyes. "Had this all planned, did you?"

"Nothing with you is planned. It just seems to happen." He cupped her chin tenderly in his warm hand. "You are much too beautiful, you know."

She spoke his name, whisper-soft, and Jake leaned toward her, his mouth brushing hers for a light, teasing moment.

"I love you," he murmured against her slightly parted lips, and Joanna echoed the words she knew she would tell him again and again. Then slipping his arms around her, he drew her close. Jake's hands rested firmly on the hollow of her back as his mouth claimed hers in an unhurried kiss she melted into until he slowly brought it to an end.

"Remember the first time we kissed?" she asked.

"Remember?" he repeated the agonizing word. "I spent two years trying to forget." He searched her eyes with the memory fresh in his mind. "Kissing you that night, Joanna...wanting you seemed like the most natural thing in the world."

Joanna's lips curved into a subtle smile. It had felt that way for her, too, she recalled clearly. Lifting her hand, she touched his cheek, and the slight narrowing of his eyes quickened her pulse. Jake's fingers were warm and strong as he caught her hand, pressing a kiss to her palm.

"It had always been you, Jo, right from the beginning. I just didn't see it until..."

"Until we kissed," she finished the statement he had failed to complete. She stared into silvery eyes that confirmed her words as Jake's hands returned to her waist, drawing her closer.

He felt her relax, settling more fully into the warmth of his arms, and he held her snugly to him. "I tried not to think about you after I left Charleston. I wanted to forget."

"There was no need to forget," she whispered through the shadows.

"But you were so young," he said with quiet regret.

"I was twenty years old then, Jake. Not a child." She tilted her head back to meet his gaze.

He looked again into the eyes that had never been far from his memory, and the pain reflected in his expression startled Joanna. "I never wanted to love someone...anyone so much that—" He paused. "Not someone so young." Jake released her suddenly and turned away, and Joanna watched his hands move to touch the cold, white porch railing rather than the love that waited by his side.

"Please, Jake." She reached for him, placing a hand on his arm. "I want to understand."

"I watched what happened with my father," he began in an unsteady voice. "I never wanted to love anyone so much that if I lost—" He stopped abruptly, standing silently for a moment.

Joanna squeezed his arm gently, wishing he would continue.

"I could see myself loving you—losing you—living my father's life all over again." He bowed his head. "He loved my mother too much."

"And she died? Are you afraid I'll die young like your mother did?" Joanna asked, her question barely audibly.

"She didn't die, Jo," came his quiet admission. "I've let people think that for so many years, sometimes I almost believe it myself."

Joanna studied Jake's shadowy profile in what little moonlight the heavens offered. "That's why there was no tombstone next to your father's," she thought aloud.

Jake nodded. "She was everything to Dad...the center of his life," he explained, slowly and deliberately. "Then one day, she left. Just walked out." He paused again and the silence seemed to last forever.

"I was only a child, but I remember the way it changed Dad. He was never the same. Never happy. Not once after that."

"I'm so sorry." Her mind flashed back to the loss of her own parents. But she had always known they loved her; they had not willingly deserted her. "How could a mother leave her little boy?"

"How could she leave the husband who loved her?" was Jake's sharp response.

It was not the deserted little boy of Jake's past that hurt the most. It was the memory of his father's heart, broken right before his eyes, that haunted him.

"She was young, Jo, like you are," Jake said with a sad shrug. "Too much younger than Dad, too young to know what she wanted in life."

Joanna leaned against him, resting her cheek on his arm. She knew exactly what she wanted. The love of this gentle man.

"All this time, since that first moment I kissed you, I've been afraid that..."

"Afraid to love me, afraid I would leave you," Joanna finished the thought.

He did not respond. He did not need to. She understood.

Joanna raised her hand, brushing his face softly with her fingertips. "I'm not like your mother, Jake. I'm young, but I know what love is. I know what I want."

He turned to search her face through stormy eyes. "It's never been like this for me," he began and then cleared his throat. "God knows, I never wanted to love anyone this way."

"But I want you to love me," Joanna pleaded as

she slid her arms around his waist and eased into his embrace. "I've waited so long."

Jake's arms closed so tightly around her, she could barely breathe, and they held each other in the early hours of a damp spring morning.

"You're shivering," he said. "Let's go inside." Jake pushed open the front door, letting the warmth from the house flow over them. He reached for the switch and turned on the dim light in the hallway. Taking one of Joanna's hands in his, he sat down on the steps leading to the second floor of the house.

Joanna sat down close beside him, her heart aching within her as she viewed the weariness in his face. The shadowy need of a shave. Eyes, warm and tender, but tired.

"You would never have come back to me, would you," Joanna stated softly, "if it hadn't been for Aunt Mae...your concern for her? You wouldn't have come back to South Carolina. Or me." She studied his face. He would not have returned. She could see it in the honesty of his eyes.

"I'd said goodbye to you once, Jo. That was difficult enough," he answered.

"But you came—"

"Mae had always treated me like a son. When her doctor called me—"

"Her doctor? Natalie Eden called you?"

Jake nodded. "She didn't think Mae would live long."

"And she knew I wouldn't tell you," Joanna responded. "I remember when she asked if I had called you. I was so upset about Aunt Mae's condition, I didn't think much about Dr. Eden's question at the time. But now, looking back on it, I think she needed an excuse to contact you.'' Joanna tilted her head a little to the side as she studied Jake's solemn expression.

"She didn't mean anything to me, Joanna."

"You wanted to marry her—"

Jake gave a quiet laugh. "Where did you get that idea?"

"From her." Joanna pulled her hand away, clasping them both in front of her. "She said you wanted her to go with you when you moved away. She told me that a few days after you'd said goodbye to me at the day care center."

Jake gave a quiet groan. "That was the hardest thing I've ever done in my life."

She stared at him. "Saying goodbye to me?"

"Yes," he answered. "You. Not Natalie Eden, not anyone else." His voice was tender, almost a murmur.

She slipped her arm through his and kissed his shoulder, her heart brimming with love.

"When Mae asked me to promise to take you home with me, I had no idea how difficult it would be having you in my life again." He tugged lightly on a lock of blond hair. "This was only meant to be temporary, you know. There wasn't supposed to be an 'us.'"

"But I'm so glad there is," she said with a softness in her tone that drew a tender smile from Jake. Leaning into him, Joanna kissed his cheek. She liked the slightly rough feel against her lips, and she watched the corners of his mouth ease down.

"Joanna, after I talked with Pastor White today, all those fears I had about loving you didn't seem so overwhelming." His eyes swept over her face. "I thought of how much I love you, how wrong I'd been not to tell you," he said gently. "No more secrets, Jo. Don't be afraid of the truth."

But the truth, she wondered. What did it entail? She'd watched several of Jake's relationships run their course in the early years of knowing him. And there was Natalie Eden. They couldn't pretend she didn't exist. For Joanna, the past had no holds on her heart. Not until Jake. But his past wouldn't be so simple.

"Being in love with someone," Joanna began, her voice shakier than she would have liked, "I suppose it's difficult to ever really forget." She let her gaze drop from his.

"Yes, it is," he agreed with certainty. "Especially when it happens only once."

Joanna glanced up. "Jake...honestly?"

"Honestly." His mouth curved into a reassuring smile. "I won't lie to you. Not about anything, Jo. I know you love me, but you need to trust me, too."

"But you were angry when you found out that Natalie was going to marry Daniel," she reminded, bitterly recalling Ina's words.

"I was jealous of both of them," he replied. "I'm tired of seeing others start out on these lifelong relationships with no worries about what tomorrow will bring," he admitted. "I knew then that I wanted a future with you, but I was too afraid to hope for it."

"I didn't know," Joanna answered. "I thought you wanted Natalie—"

"No, I wasn't interested in her. Nothing happened between Natalie and me. Nothing. I let you think there was something between us for a while only because I wanted you to forget me. To get on with your life.''

"But I could never forget you."

He reached for her hand, grazing her knuckles with a kiss. "If you had, I'd be a lost soul. In every way imaginable." But he could see the uncertainty in her eyes. The doubts that lingered. "I know there are times that Natalie stretches the truth for her own convenience, but I promise you, Joanna, I did not ask her to marry me or to move back here with me. In fact, I suggested that she consider moving to Indianapolis to go into practice with Daniel. He's been in love with her for years."

"Why didn't you tell me sooner? I thought *you* were in love with her." And because of that Joanna had told Ina she was leaving, she remembered clearly. Jake had heard her say it. "I did exactly the thing you'd been afraid I would do, didn't I? I left."

Jake didn't reply. He didn't need to. The pain in his eyes was the only confirmation she needed.

"Oh, how could I have done that?" she asked. "I ran away from you, from what we had together."

"I wanted to explain, but you said you were leaving. All I could think of was my father...."

"I'm sorry," she moaned, leaning her head against his shoulder. "I'm so sorry, Jake. I was just so hurt, so jealous."

Jake kissed the top of her head. "You had no reason to be. There's no one you need be jealous of." He hesitated. "Look at me, Jo."

She tilted her face to do as he asked, and he saw her questioning eyes, so young and innocent. He

touched her forehead in a light kiss and looked away.
He was thirty-four years old. He'd lived most of those
years doing whatever he pleased, and Joanna knew
that. She knew the man he had been as well as she
knew the changed man he was tonight, sitting with
her now. "I can't undo the past, Joanna. God knows
I would, if I could."

Joanna blinked hard, resisting the tears welling up
in her eyes. Jake slipped his arms around her and held
her close.

"You're everything good and lovely and...I have
no idea why God would allow you to love me the
way you do."

Her tears overflowed. "Jake, don't say—"

"It's true. You deserve far better." He paused,
hugging her tighter and pressing his mouth against
her temple in a kiss. His warm breath stirred her hair.
"But, for some reason, He's entrusting you to me and
I'll be grateful to Him for the rest of my life. What
I'm trying to tell you is...I love you, more than I can
say. I always will." How he wanted this woman. To
have and to hold. From this day on. "Joanna—"

Just then the phone rang. Loudly. They both looked
toward the intrusive noise.

Joanna's hand flew to her mouth. "I forgot to call
Aaron." She stood up and hurried to the phone.
"Hello. Barb? Yes, we're okay," she said and continued on with the conversation while Jake watched
her, studying her changing expressions as she spoke
to Barbara.

"No, no, it wasn't Jake's plane. He's safe...he's
fine. I know it's against the rules to ask this so late,
Barb, but could I talk to Aaron for a minute?"

"I wish you would," Barbara replied. "No one else can do much with him tonight. Hold on."

Joanna could hear Aaron's little bare feet padding across the floor. Then he grabbed up the receiver, fumbling with it noisily against the desk.

"Jo-Jo? Are you okay?"

"Yes, honey, everything is okay," she answered, smiling at the sound of his sleepy voice.

Aaron sniffed loudly. "You left—"

"I know I did, and I'm sorry that it scared you. It was something I had to do. I didn't have any choice."

"Yep. Kinda like me being in that play tonight?" He sniffed again.

"Yes, exactly." She laughed softly. "You didn't have any choice about being a sunflower, and I didn't have any choice about going to the airport tonight. I was worried about Jake, and I had to find him."

"Is Doc there? Was he crashed in the plane like Freddie said?"

"No, sweetie, Doc's fine," Joanna responded, and her eyes followed Jake down the staircase as he moved toward her. "He's right here with me, Aaron."

"Yes," Jake agreed quietly as he approached her with the hint of a smile on his lips. "Doc is right here where he wants to be," he added, gently pushing a handful of blond hair away from her neck. His mouth felt moist and warm against her skin.

"Come see me, Jo-Jo. You and Doc."

Joanna could feel her own pulse beating in her throat as delicious sensations shot through her. "It's too late tonight, Aaron," she replied with some difficulty, "but tomorrow we'll come out to see you."

Jake abandoned the softness of Joanna's neck and slid an arm around her. "Let me talk to him," he said, lifting the phone from her hand. "Hello, champ. How are you?"

"Okay, but when you weren't here tonight, I got real scared something happened to you."

"No, I'm all right. There was a problem at the airport, and I had to stay for a while. I'm sorry I missed your play."

"That's okay. Sometimes you gotta help people because you're a doctor."

"I'll make it up to you. I'll try to come to the next one you're in."

"If I'm lucky, I won't ever have to be in any more dumb plays. I hate bein' a sunflower," Aaron responded.

"Sunflower, huh?" Jake repeated while Joanna tenderly traced the angular line of his jaw with one finger. "I'll bet you were the best sunflower in the bunch."

"I was the only one that got to talk."

Jake laughed quietly. "Good for you, Aaron. Maybe you can say your lines for us tomorrow. Jo-Jo and I will be out to see you after lunch, but it's late now. You'd better get back to bed."

"Okay, good night, Doc."

Joanna took the receiver, "Aaron?"

"Good night, Jo-Jo."

"Sleep well. We'll see you tomorrow."

"Yep. See ya then."

Barbara instantly was on the other end of the phone. "Joanna! I've got a message for you that you're not going to believe! I just found it here on the desk. It's from some woman who said she worked at the ticket counter at the airport.''

Jake turned his attention to Joanna's mouth, touching the corner of her smile with a warm thumb.

"A message?" Joanna responded.

Jake's eyes brightened. "Ask her to read it to you.''

Joanna searched his gaze, wondering about that sudden glint of amusement she'd found there. "Barbara, what does it say?''

"You'd better sit down for this. Are you sure you're ready?''

It was more suspense than Joanna could tolerate. "Barb, just read it.''

"Here goes…it says, and I quote, 'Jake said to tell you it wasn't his plane. He's all right, and he wants to marry you.' Joanna, this man wants to marry you!''

Jake smiled at her, his fingers touching her ear as he tucked away a stray curl. His voice, infinitely tender, nearly melted her heart. "Will you?''

"Yes, Jake. Yes,'' she said through fresh tears of happiness. "I thought you'd never ask.''

"Joanna?'' Barbara's voice interrupted them. "This guy wants to marry you! I thought you just sort of rented a room from him or something.''

"So did I.'' Joanna smiled at the man she knew she would love for the rest of her life. And beyond.

Jake drew her close.

"But, Joanna,'' Barbara persisted. "What about this message? This is pretty rare. Do you want me to save it for you? Don't you want to read it?''

"Barb,'' she began as Jake's hand closed over the phone. He tugged it away from Joanna's hand, holding it several inches from her. His gaze, devastatingly direct, offered the promise of all their tomorrows. "I don't need to read the message," Joanna added quietly. "I can see it in his eyes."

"Goodbye, Barbara," Jake added before the receiver went back into place.

"Marry me, Jo," he whispered before his mouth settled over hers in a kiss more possessive than any she'd known. And nothing felt more right than being in this man's arms.

"When?" she asked after she caught her breath.

"Tomorrow. The next day. However soon we can arrange it."

Joanna's eyes shone with pleasure. "I love you, Jake. I love you, I love you, I love you."

"And you'll never leave," he stated, not wanting to hear those words spoken as a question. A possibility. He was trusting her with his heart, his life. Everything.

"Never," she promised. "Never. There's a Bible verse that says, 'The boundary lines have fallen for me in pleasant places.' And they have for me. I've waited for years to discover that the Lord has allowed you to be within my boundaries. I'm not going anywhere without you," she assured him and watched his mouth slant into a familiar smile. The warmth returned to his gaze.

"There is one place I need you to go without me." He cupped her chin tenderly in his warm hand. "To your room for the night." His smile widened. "And lock the door."

"Don't trust me?" Joanna teased.

"I don't trust *me*," Jake answered emphatically.

"A day or two, Joanna. Then you'll be my wife. I'm going to do this the right way, God's way, even if it kills me," he added with a quick kiss to her forehead. "Now, go."

She laughed softly. A couple of days could feel like a long time, but sometimes God takes the long way around, she'd learned. At least it seemed that way, this side of heaven. This time the journey had taken her from South Carolina, right into the heart of Indiana...and Jake Barnes. And Joanna couldn't think of any place she'd rather be for the next hundred years or so.

* * * * *

Dear Reader,

The story of Joanna Meccord and Jake Barnes is a favorite of mine. I couldn't help but feel sorry for Joanna, loving a man who wouldn't let himself love her in return. What a cold and lonely existence Jake had mapped out for himself. If he hadn't learned to see past the mistakes of others and trust God for guidance in his life, there could not have been a happy ending to this story.

God can meet each of us at our point of need. Whether we're like Jake, well into adult life when he finally realizes God loves him, or more like Joanna, who has been a Christian for years but finds herself going through ups and downs—in *any* situation, God can meet us there. And when He does, He can make something beautiful of our lives.

May God bless you!

Kathryn Alexander